White KNIGHT

Book Two of the Dirty Mafia Duet

MEGHAN

MARCH

Copyright © 2019 by Meghan March LLC

All rights reserved.

Editor: Pam Berehulke, Bulletproof Editing

Cover Design: Murphy Rae, www.murphyrae.com

Visit my website at www.meghanmarch.com

I never expected to be anyone's white knight. That's not a
role I've ever played.
But when the Casso crime family shifts into uncharted
territory, they're looking for a new hero, and they're
looking for me—Cannon Freeman, the black sheep.
But my time in disgrace is at an end.
It's my turn to rise up and save the people who matter
most to me.
Even if my family has never given a damn about me, I will
not let them fall.
More than anything, I will not let her fall.
One thing I know is true—in my life, nothing is ever what
it seems.

White Knight is the second book in the Dirty Mafia Duet
and should be read after *Black Sheep*, book one.

CHAPTER ONE

CANNON

Twenty-five years earlier

Even the weather got the memo that today was the crappiest day ever to hit the city. The dark gray skies spat rain and snow as the limo driver crawled his way down the street, even with a police escort.

That's right, a police escort, and they weren't even taking us to jail or to court. No, they took us to the cemetery on Staten Island where Mom's casket would be buried six feet under. I refused to think about her in that box. I didn't care that all the capos' wives said Dominic Casso had gone above and beyond, picking out that fancy, shiny wood and pink satin interior himself.

The burn of rage flared inside me like a dumpster fire.

If she hadn't still been trying to win him back, no one would have targeted her. He's the reason she's dead.

It was the God's honest truth, and every single person on their way to this ridiculous funeral knew it. He'd killed her just as sure as if he'd pulled the trigger himself, unleashing the hail of bullets that tore through her and left her bleeding out on those steps.

I slammed my eyes shut when the memory of her blood seeping into the cracks of the concrete stole into my mind. It didn't help.

I opened them to look into the face of the man who was responsible for the death of the only parent who'd claim me, except Dom wasn't looking at me. He was staring out the window, probably wondering how soon he could leave and get back to business. Because everything was business to him. Even this.

"Watch him, Cannon. You'll learn so much, and it'll open so many doors for you. Just trust me on this."

Mom had been naive at nineteen when Dom swept her off her feet, and she was even more naive the day she died —because she still believed in love and miracles and happily ever after. *How the hell was that even possible?*

Dom's face turned and his enigmatic eyes drilled into me. "I can feel your fucking rage from over here, kid. You know I took care of it."

Dom's gruff voice sounded exactly like it always did. It wasn't hoarse from grief due to the solemn occasion playing out today. Of course not. Because a man like Dominic Casso wasn't capable of tears. Wasn't capable of giving a single damn that a woman who loved him more than life itself was gunned down on his goddamned stoop.

My jaw tightened as I tried to pull it together, or at least bury my feelings and slap a mask of indifference over them.

But I couldn't.

"She was my mother," I said from between clenched teeth. "Someone killed her. In cold blood. Because of *you*."

My nostrils flared and my fingers curled into fists. I wanted to throw myself across the back seat of the limo and bloody my knuckles destroying his face until the driver slammed on the brakes and ripped me out of the car. They'd probably put a bullet in me and leave me for dead. Just like Mom.

But I didn't do it.

Because Mom wouldn't have wanted that. There was nothing I could do that would go against her wishes more than causing that kind of trouble for myself.

"Be the smart, sweet boy we both know you are, and he won't be able to help but love you. He'll see that you're different. You're meant for big things."

Mom had such high hopes for my future, but I didn't share even a flicker of the optimism she had. *Future,* I scoffed silently. *What the hell was that now?*

I finally lifted my eyes to Dom once more, but his gaze hadn't wavered an inch.

With his arm against the door, he held his chin as he spoke. "What you're feeling right now? Embrace it. Hold it. Remember it. Don't you ever fucking forget how this moment feels. To have something taken from you before you were ready to give it up is the ultimate insult."

Dom glanced out the window, but my attention snagged on the clenched hand at his side. He straightened his fingers twice before locking them together in a fist. When his eyes came back to me, they were teeming with wrath.

"And then the next time someone wrongs you, you

reach down inside and grab hold of this feeling with both hands, and you *use it*."

Right now, all I wanted to do was seize that fury and use it to end him.

Dom leaned back against the leather and unbuttoned and rebuttoned his jacket. Normally, he was a man who wasted no movement, but today he couldn't seem to sit still. Maybe he wasn't totally unaffected by all this.

"You always were a mama's boy, kid."

My entire body tensed, my prior thought brushed away as soon as he spoke, but he either didn't care or notice and kept going.

"That shit wasn't gonna get you anywhere in this life or the next, so you look at this as an opportunity. Not a loss."

He did not just say that. But the man kept talking, straightening his shoulders and staring me down.

"Harness that anger and learn to become your own fucking man. No more mama to run to when shit gets bad. Figure it out yourself. Rely on yourself. Have loyalty to me and no one else other than *yourself*. You hear me, kid?"

I wouldn't have been able to miss the bark behind his words even if I shoved my head out of the window of this moving limo, which I didn't, but I wanted to. I didn't want to hear this shit. Not from him. Not now. Not ever.

The words *go screw yourself* hung on my tongue, but my mom's innocent voice echoed through my mind.

"Please don't ruin this day for me. This is the last time I'll ever see how much he loved me. You can see it, right, Cannon?

He really loved me. It didn't matter that he never left his wife. He loved me."

The earnest tone my mother's ghost used to speak in my ear was enough to make me wish I had one of those guns all the Casso men carried so I could send Dom off to tell Mom in person how much he loved her. But I couldn't. I'd never shot a gun. I didn't want to be like them. I didn't want to deal out death when I was wronged —with exception of this long, cold car ride.

I wanted a normal life. Friends at school. To play sports. To be part of something that wasn't the *mob*.

But you didn't always get what you wanted. I knew that now more than ever. The only thing I truly needed was my mom back in our apartment, her hair curled and lipstick on, even as she whipped up dinner.

Something I could never have again.

Dominic Casso would never be my father. No, he'd only ever be the man who got my mother killed.

I would never be like him. Not as long as I lived.

CHAPTER TWO

CANNON

Present day

"I*t's time to prove yourself. You take care of her, or I will."*

The moment I've been waiting for over half my life has finally come. *Him or me.* Dominic Casso's fingers wrap around the barrel of his Sig and he shoves the grip toward me, like he's expecting me to take it and put a bullet in a woman.

After all these years, he still doesn't know jack shit about me.

I may have been born a mobster's bastard, but I'm not a fucking mobster. Regardless, I learned at the feet of one of the best, so I relax my posture and study him lazily.

Rule number one: never let them see you sweat, even if you don't have a single fucking clue how the hell you're going to get out of the situation without dying or ending up covered in blood spatter.

"In a construction site? Isn't that a little cliché?" I ask, injecting as much indolence into my tone as I possibly can. Dom hates it, but I've never given a damn what he likes.

He's not taking another person from me, despite the fact that she probably hasn't given me a word of truth since the second we met. But that's not the point.

The point is that *I* am the one who will decide how this situation will be handled. No one else. I won't let Dom take another decision out of my hands. Not now and not ever again.

No doubt a therapist would say there's still a hell of a lot of that enraged kid rolling around inside me.

"I don't give a fuck where you do it, but it's time. I'm done fucking around with this shit," Dom says, shoving the gun toward me again. "Do it, or I will. Your choice, but believe me that I will remember which one you fucking choose."

Fingers curl into the back of my suit jacket. The touch of my betrayer. The woman who got us into this situation to begin with. The one who I would be a fool to trust now. And an even bigger fool if I were to choose her over the only family I've known for most of my life.

"Time to be your own man," Dom told me once. I'm pretty sure he didn't mean for me to remember that right now, when he's offering me a gun and a choice I didn't ask to make.

Before I can make a move, Primo, one of Dom's ever-present bodyguards, shuts the passenger side door of the SUV and walks around the back to pop the tailgate. That's when I hear muffled screaming.

My gaze cuts between Primo and Dom. "What the fuck is going on?"

One of Dom's steel-gray eyebrows rises like he doesn't get why I'm confused, but he doesn't say anything.

In my mind, all I can picture is Memphis's stepmother being hauled out of the SUV and dragged toward us. My blood, already running cold, slogs along in my veins.

But I'm wrong.

It's not Cynthia Lockwood. It's someone completely different.

As soon as Primo gets the woman out of the back and carries her across the gravel construction site, kicking and screaming and with her hands bound in front of her, a wave of relief washes over me.

Teal.

Holy. Fucking. Shit.

Thankful I have one hell of a poker face, I mask every single thought I'm having in this moment. If Dom knew what was going through my head, he'd empty the entire magazine into my chest and tell Primo to bury me under an ocean of concrete where no one would find my body.

From behind me, I hear a swiftly inhaled breath, and I pray like I haven't prayed in years that Drew—*Memphis*—keeps her fucking mouth shut.

With that prayer sent up, I return my attention to Dom, who is watching Teal as she's brought closer. Her mascara runs down her face in black streaks. She was probably fucked up when they found her.

"Ms. Fancy Tits here thinks she can go wherever the fuck she wants and run her mouth about my business," Dom says with his lip curled.

Teal's short party dress rides up as she struggles in Primo's hold. The terror on her face as she tries to squirm free strikes a chord of pity inside me. Finally, she's sober and very fucking aware of the consequences of her actions.

I've been trying to get through to her for months to make her understand that life isn't a fucking game. She couldn't keep expecting her sister to cover for her while she fucked off, making us all look bad. Which was when I started cutting her shifts, letting her work just enough while I found a replacement. Tanya was supposed to break the news to her that she was fired, but we both know how that went sideways. I still can't get Teal's meltdown in the break room out of my head.

I was brutally honest with her then. She didn't take it well.

Now here she is, her blue eyes full of tears, pleading for me to help her. Again. Except this time, she must have gotten mixed up in something new and different for Dom to want her dead.

"What did she do?" Feigning indifference, I slowly shift my head and keep the weight of the moment out of my tone.

"Got smashed at one of Gabriel Legend's underground clubs she gets into *using my name* and then runs into that fucking Rossetti punk, Donny Linetti." Dom's furrowed face takes on a ruddier hue. "From the video footage we've already hacked, he cornered her and she started talking. Saying shit about *my organization*."

All the hair on the back of my neck stands up as Dom recounts Teal's cardinal sin. *Fucking hell.* The only thing I can't figure out is why the hell he brought her to me, because for that, she should already be dead.

I wait in silence for Dom to continue.

"Donny starts to drag her out of the club, and Legend, that fucking upstart who's out to prove he's king shit, intervenes and kicks out the Rossetti crew. *And then she uses my fucking name again* with Legend as a get-out-of-jail-free card. He had her brought to my brownstone this morning, with a bow and a note that said I owed him a fucking favor now for saving one of my girls' asses. Do you believe that shit? The audacity of that fucking bitch and that punk?"

The lines between Dom's eyebrows deepen as his temper flares and his teeth grind together.

Oh. Fuck.

"I don't hand out favors unless *I want to.*" Dom turns and taps the butt of the Sig he offered to me against Teal's temple. "You hear me, little girl? You fucking cost me, and I didn't give you leave to cost me shit. And that doesn't even begin to cover whatever information you might have given to the fucking Rossettis. You caught your last chance, girl. Now you're done."

Teal crumples, sobbing hard as tears roll down her cheeks. I know she can cry on demand, but this isn't that. This is knowing you fucked up and you're going to die.

And yet I hear myself saying, "She has a problem. She needs help, Dom, not a fucking bullet to the head."

Words spill from Teal's lips as she drops to her knees, her fingers gripping the fine weave of Dom's suit pants. "I didn't tell him anything, I swear. I didn't. I don't know anything. I don't. I was fucked up. I swear whatever I told him was bullshit."

Dom shakes her off and steps away, his fingers still wrapped around the barrel of the Sig. Before he shifts his grip to where he can pull the trigger, I have the urge to snatch it out of his hand. *I'm not like him.* I won't let him execute Teal right here, right now.

And then there's the reason I thought he was hunting me down. *Drew.* No, *Memphis.*

She and I aren't in the clear yet either. At best, we've gotten a mere stay of execution. While Dom's not looking, I reach behind me and find her cold fingers, giving them a quick squeeze before jamming my hand in my pocket.

I hope like hell she knows to stay quiet and let me do all the talking, because that's the only way any of the three of us are making it out of this construction site alive. And the only way I'll ever be able to find out what the fuck she was thinking when she slipped right into my life like she belonged.

Did she belong? Was any of it real? Obviously, now isn't the time for that conversation, but I'm going to make sure we have it, goddammit. Dom isn't stealing that from me too.

"Why should I believe a goddamned word out of your mouth, bitch? You'd say anything right now to save your own ass."

"I swear I don't know anything worth telling anyone, whether you believe me or not." Teal's voice catches on her sobs as her shoulders droop in defeat.

Dom's dark gaze cuts to me. "And you think she needs *help*? Like she should get another fucking chance after all this? She uses and abuses *my name*, costs me a *favor*, and you think the right answer is getting her some *help*?"

I hear it clearly in his tone—Dom thinks I'm a pussy, which is fine for now if it saves Teal's life. I might have been pissed off enough to fire her, but I'm not a fucking murderer.

Dom fits the Sig's grip into his palm like he's done thousands of times before and presses the barrel against her forehead. Only, I know better. This whole fucking thing is about proving a point. He won't use his own piece, not on her and not for wet work. If someone puts a bullet in Teal's head, it'll come from Primo's throwaway, which will be wiped clean before it's tossed.

"One round is all it'll take. Sixty-seven cents. That's it. That's what your life has come down to." He jabs the metal harder. "Do you think your life is worth more than sixty-seven cents, girl?"

Teal's tears tumble faster as she blinks rapidly, probably because she's afraid to nod her head. I'm surprised she hasn't fainted.

"She needs to go to rehab," I say.

Dom's quick glare would carve me in half if I wasn't so used to being on the receiving end of his rage. "Rehab costs money. No one gets help for free around here. Especially not ungrateful little bitches who use my name, spill information, and then *cost me favors.*" Another nudge of the barrel against the bridge of her nose. "So, you tell me, Teal. What the fuck should I do with you? Because you're not even worth sixty-seven cents to me right now."

"I'll pay for her rehab," I say before I even plan to form the words. It's like someone plucked them out of thin air and shoved them in my mouth before I could even decide to say them. Because if I'd been thinking, I'd have said that her health insurance from the club is good through the end of the month and should cover the cost.

But I don't add that detail because Dom jerks around to face me, the pistol still touching Teal. "You'll pay for it? Why? She ain't worth it. I can tell you that right now."

How do you explain the value of human life to a man who has never understood it before? You can't.

"Let me worry about that."

Dom's gaze narrows. "You already got a piece of ass that's so hot you plan to fuck her in a construction site. What do you need with a whore who'll spread her legs for anyone? You're better than that shit."

I dig down deep, into the cold, dead part of me that's descended from this man. "You kill her, I'll have her sister to deal with, and I need good, loyal—*quiet*—employees. They're fucking hard to find."

It's a practical, emotionless reason. One I know Dom will understand.

His lower lip rises, pressing against the top. "You *sure* her sister's really worth the cost of rehab? Because if she makes a fuss, we'll take care of her too."

Fucking hell.

Dom would never ask a mobster if he's *sure*. It means he thinks I'm weak, and that's not saving Teal—or Tanya.

It's a dangerous move, but I know the callous man before me. I know what he respects and what he hates, so I stare him down.

"Did I stutter, Dom? I'll cover the cost. Now, let's get back to fucking business. I've got shit to do today."

Better men have been killed for less than what I just said to him, but the corner of his mouth curls up and respect gleams in his eyes. Like he's finally seeing his likeness in me.

Not a fucking chance.

Then again, you don't get to choose your DNA.

CHAPTER THREE

"You're a good man," I whisper to Cannon as Teal whimpers from the back seat of the Chevelle.

He turns his head to glance at me, and his features are so hard, they may as well have been stamped in flint. Sweat dots his brow, and his neck is flushed an angry crimson.

"Now is not the time you want to be making assumptions about me." He looks back at the road, slowing to a stop as the light turns red, and the only sound in the car is Teal's snuffling. It's the longest red light of my life.

There are a million things I want to say. Starting with . . .

Thank you for not taking the gun and shooting me.

Thank you for not ratting me out to your mob boss dad.

Thank you for protecting this girl I don't even know, but she's obviously young and stupid.

But I say none of it. We drive back to the club without another word passing between us.

As soon as we drive into the garage, Tanya is at the

passenger door, ripping it open and pushing her head past me to see into the back seat.

"Thank God. Thank God," she whispers as she reaches out to touch Teal's rat's nest of a hairstyle.

As she maneuvers around me, I say, "I'll . . . um . . . get out and you can—"

Tanya's blue eyes frost over as they land on mine. "Move."

"Tanya." Cannon says her name like a bark as he climbs out and slams the door. "What the fuck happened? You told me you had it taken care of. You told me that you were getting her help. What. The. Fuck?" His voice echoes off the concrete walls, but he doesn't seem to care who hears.

Tanya squeezes her eyes shut before she removes her head from the Chevelle and steps back so I can exit. As soon as I'm out of the car, I march around to the hood, not wanting to be caught in the cross fire.

"We picked out a place last night," Tanya says quietly, her fingertips resting on the roof. "They said they had room to take her. She asked me if we could spend this afternoon together and I'd put her on the train tonight. The staff was going to pick her up and get her settled. I really thought she meant it. I swear." Her attention cuts to the interior as Teal sobs louder.

"I'm sorry, Tanny. I'm so sorry. I only wanted one more night out, just to prove that I didn't really need help. That I could handle myself." Teal doesn't even sound like she believes herself.

Every feature on Tanya's face freezes into a hard expression I thought she only reserved for me. "You *lied* to me?" Her question is whispered with such quiet, lethal force, it could slice a woman to shreds.

Tanya bends at the waist and yanks the car seat forward so she can reach into the back and drag her younger sister out by her messy hair. "Are you fucking serious right now?"

"I'm sorry!" the other girl wails. "You were right. I need help. I'm sick."

Tanya shakes her sister by the shoulder, and I inch toward Cannon without even thinking.

"I told you we were getting you help, and then you pull this shit on *me*, the one person who would literally do anything for you? How? Why?" Like she knows she won't get an answer that matters, Tanya keeps going. "Do you know how fucking terrified I was when I went to get you, and you were gone and your roommate said that you went out last night to a Legend club? And then when I called in every favor I could to find you today, I found out they delivered you to *Dom* after you'd been with one of the Rossetti crew last night? What the hell is the matter with you? Are you trying to get yourself killed?"

Someone clears his throat from behind us. I shoot a glance over my shoulder to see Warren walking in our direction slowly enough for us to realize he's there and not feel like he's not eavesdropping. But from the look on his face, it's obvious he's most definitely catching every word we say.

"What place did you pick out, Tanya?" Cannon asks, but his gaze is on Warren and not the head waitress.

"It's in Albany. Not too fancy, and not too skid row. I'll take her there right now. I was going to track her ass down and take her there today, whether she wanted to go or not. I swear." Tanya pleads her case, her fingers trembling as they rake through her hair.

Cannon nods at Warren. "You're taking them to Albany. Bring Tanya back to the club when it's done." He stalks around the car, passing me like I'm not even there, and stops in front of Tanya. "You're working the late shift tonight. I don't fucking care that I gave you the day off. You are so goddamned lucky that your sister isn't in a shallow grave with a bullet in her head. Remember that, and work your fucking ass off to say thank you. No more attitude. No more bullshit." He leans in closer, but his voice doesn't get any less threatening when he asks, "Do you fucking get me?"

Tanya couldn't have possibly nodded faster. Her head was already bobbing before Cannon was finished speaking.

"I get you. I'm sorry. Thank you. Seriously, thank you. I don't know what I would do—"

He lifts his hand in the air, halting her. "I don't want to hear it. This conversation is over. I'll see you tonight." With that, Cannon strides toward the elevator. "Hurry up, *Drew*. Time to get to fucking work."

CHAPTER FOUR

CANNON

I'm a stupid fucking idiot. I wouldn't be bringing the fox back into the henhouse *on purpose* if I wasn't. Then again, if I fired her on the spot, Dom would know something was up, and then I'd actually have the situation on my hands that I only thought I had earlier.

"It's time to prove yourself. You take care of her, or I will."

It's been a long damn time since words could send a cold chill through my blood. Even the words of a man who is more than capable of murder. But the whole time, it wasn't me I was worried about.

I jab the elevator button as soon as she steps inside, then sneak a sideways glare at her.

When the door closes, I'm tempted to slam the EMERGENCY STOP button and ask her *what the fuck*, but I can't do that either. I know for a fact the elevator is bugged.

I have a million fucking questions for this woman, starting with *Do you have a death wish?* But I can't ask her a single one of them until we get out of here tonight.

"I'm sorry," Memphis whispers from beside me.

Something seizes in my chest as I jerk my chin in her direction. She's pale beneath the thick layer of makeup on her face. The thick layer that was her disguise as she tried to gather intel, probably to put me in prison with the rest of the Casso crew.

And I fucking fell for it hook, line, and sinker. No, I fucking fell for her. What a goddamned schmuck.

"Don't say a fucking word about anything until I tell you it's okay to talk. Understand me?" My words are sharp, no care to them at all.

She flinches, but I won't apologize as easily as she does. It's not just Teal's life I'm saving today. It's hers too.

As the elevator opens on the floor for the Upper Ten, I step over the threshold and block her exit. Memphis stares at me with genuine fear on her face as she swallows.

"Your mother expects you to take her to dinner tonight. Tell her you're working, and you'll take her tomorrow. No one gets the fucking night off today."

I should want her as far away from the club as possible, but I'm not letting Memphis Lockwood out of my sight until I figure out what kind of voodoo she's worked on me, and what the fuck I'm going to do about it.

Her mouth forms an *o*, like she wants to speak, but she nods rather than replying.

I fish her cell phone out of my pocket and toss it to her before I turn and stalk away. The elevator doors close with her inside as I brush past Grice without a word.

CHAPTER FIVE

I dodged a bullet. A really, really big one that should have had at least one of my names engraved on the side.

As the elevator doors open once more on the floor for the Upper Ten, shivers rack my body like someone just tap-danced over my grave. Maybe it's my father's ghost warning me, trying to protect me from my own recklessness. He always told me to be careful, more careful than I would ever think to be. He was right, and I should have listened.

Then again, look where his need for the truth got him. Like father, like daughter.

Shaking off the chill, I make my way toward the door, which Grice opens with a questioning look on his face.

"Everything okay, Ms. Carson?" His thick New York accent seems even more pronounced today. "Anything you need help with?" He shifts his weight as if anxiously awaiting some very bad news. *Like Teal being dead.*

Oh Lord. It's not my place to say a single word, but the

look on his face engenders so much empathy that I can't go on letting him wonder.

"Tanya had to take care of something. Cannon asked her to work the late shift tonight . . . *after her sister is settled at her new place.*" I whisper the last bit, hoping it will offer him some comfort.

Immediately, his shoulders relax and his entire posture changes. He glances up at the ceiling and makes a quick sign of the cross, like he just touched holy water at church.

When he meets my gaze once more, he smiles softly. "Thank you, Ms. Carson. I'll be pulling a double today, so I'll make sure to watch out for her coming back." He swings the interior door to the club open and lets me walk through.

Cannon is nowhere to be seen, but Letty is running entrées out to a table seated for an early dinner and her brows jump to her hairline when she sees me.

I hurry toward the kitchen, intending to check on what else needs to go out, but Matteo, the club's cigar sommelier, stops me next to the bar.

"Is Teal okay? We heard . . . things." Matteo's normally precisely starched shirt has a few wrinkles, as if he rushed out the door in yesterday's uniform because he was in such a hurry to get here, and his cheeks are paler than normal.

Apparently, everyone got the emergency call and came running in.

I nod in response, biting my lip, because I'm not sure what else I should say to him. Probably nothing. But that doesn't stop me from saying, "Tanya will be back with

Warren late tonight. I'm sure she'll be able to give you the whole story."

The warm hue of his tanned skin returns as he takes a deep breath. "Okay. Got it. That makes sense."

"Matteo."

When Cannon shouts the man's name, Matteo spins around to face our very unhappy-looking boss.

"Yes, Mr. Freeman?"

"You're not supposed to be here until seven. If you want to stay, fine. But I'll need you late tonight too. You decide if you want to work all the hours or just some."

Matteo straightens and lifts his chin. "I'm here for the duration, Mr. Freeman. I've already sold several nice sticks this afternoon, and I think it's going to be a great day for business."

Cannon's dark expression doesn't shift. "Fine. Get to work. Ms. Carson has plenty to do being the only server we have for a while."

Matteo scurries off, and Cannon stares hard at me for several long seconds before shaking his head and spinning around to return to his office.

The sight of him walking away hits me harder than it should. My eyes sting as I think of everything I've fucked up.

I wasn't supposed to feel things.

I wasn't supposed to fall for him.

What the hell do I do now?

My father's rules of investigating didn't cover what happens when you fall for the target and he finds out you lied to him and now hates your guts.

Before I can dwell on the situation any longer, a hand

lands on my shoulder. I jerk away and stare up at Silas Bohannon's face in shock.

"Sorry, I thought you heard me say your name."

Gathering myself quickly, I straighten like Matteo did and paste a smile on my face. "I'm so sorry, Mr. Bohannon. I didn't realize you were still here. What can I get for you? Another drink? Something to eat? A smoking room and Matteo?"

His eyes narrow on me, roving over my face like he recognizes my mask and is trying to see behind it. "A bottle of mineral water, and a Band-Aid for my ego."

Confused, I pull my head back and stare up at him. "Excuse me, sir?"

"You're totally blind to every man in the room when he's around. Dangerous business to have a thing for your boss. Especially when it's Cannon Freeman."

"Uh, wh-what?" My dumbfounded tone and stuttering reply probably match my dazed expression.

"Don't worry about it. Just . . . be careful, Drew. I don't know how much you know about your boss, but you might want to learn a little more before you go racing down that road."

We both turn to look in the direction Cannon just disappeared in, but he's already through the hidden door.

I clear my throat and give Silas a smile that can't possibly appear sincere. "It's a little late for warnings at this point." It's nice to know that I'm capable of speaking the truth . . . apparently, just not when it counts.

His brow furrows and a moment later, he pulls something out of his pocket and hands it to me. It's a card with the initials *S.B.* and a number on it.

"I probably shouldn't offer, but if you ever need anything, or ever get yourself into trouble . . . I spend a lot of time in the city, and I'm damn good at keeping secrets." His gaze sharpens as I tuck the card into my pocket. "And I also watched a lot of the Investigation Network when I was studying for my last role."

That's when I realize what I'm seeing on his face is knowledge. *He's feeling me out to see if his suspicions are right, and whether I'll admit I'm not who I say I am.* A chunk of ice in the form of a ticking time bomb forms in my stomach.

Stay cool. Act cool. Be cool. My mantra repeats in my head.

"Thank you for the offer, Mr. Bohannon. I'm sure I'll be fine. I'll get you that mineral water, and please let me know if there's anything else you need."

He gives me a slow nod and returns to his seat.

That feeling of someone walking over my grave? It's back with a vengeance.

CHAPTER SIX

CANNON

I've been watching her on the security cameras like I'm some kind of degenerate stalker. My fingers itch to look her up online now that I know her real name, but I won't. Dom has access to the same security footage I do, and it wouldn't be hard to zoom in on my computer screen.

Since taking over the club, I've lived in a world that's the equivalent of a fishbowl, but it never really bothered me until now, when I want to order Memphis Lockwood into my office and demand a complete explanation for what the hell is going on. I glance at the clock again, hyperaware that only ten minutes have passed since the last time I checked the time.

Why today of all days? When I can't leave and take her with me and say fuck this place and everyone in it?

Because that's life. Always putting obstacles in front of the things you truly want, just to test your resolve. My patience is strong, but this afternoon it's getting the workout of the century.

I will get my answers, and I'll get them today. Or rather, in the early hours of tomorrow, when I'm finally able to escort her back to my place for an interrogation that will do the Spanish Inquisition proud.

With that decision settled, I glance back at the security cameras again and still. Silas Bohannon, hotshot actor extraordinaire, has her cornered. He's handing her something. *What the fuck?*

Drew—no, *Memphis*—scurries away to the kitchen while tucking a card in her pocket.

What the hell? Is he part of her scam? Is she here to get information on him *and not the family?*

Or is she already moving on to new territory and getting ready to jump ship?

Over my dead fucking body.

Despite the anger that's been rolling through me at a steady boil today, a spike of jealousy pierces my chest. My hands curl into fists as I shove back in my chair. Less than sixty seconds later, I'm standing beside Bohannon's table.

"Mr. Bohannon, why don't you have a cigar with me? On the house. I've got something I'd like to discuss with you."

Memphis approaches the table, a green bottle of Perrier clutched in her hand, and she trips on a nonexistent wrinkle in the carpet when she hears me.

Bohannon looks up at me, assessing and suspicious.

Memphis silently places the bottle on the table and then backs away, and Bohannon's attention goes with her before cutting back to me. He doesn't respond until she disappears into the kitchen again.

"I have a feeling I know what you want to talk about,"

he says, relaxing deep into the leather chair and threading his fingers together on his lap. "But you're barking up the wrong tree. I'm not trespassing on your territory, Freeman. Just offering assistance if it happens to be needed."

All I see is red.

"If you'd like to retain your membership in this club, I suggest you keep your offers of assistance to yourself."

Instead of looking shocked or insulted, he throws his head back and laughs.

What the fuck is so goddamned funny? I grind my teeth silently as I wait for him to speak.

"Oh, you've got it bad, man. I only recognize it because I've been there. Hell, I'm still there. It ain't fun either."

I glance around us out of habit before I lower myself into the chair across from him. "What the fuck are you talking about?"

He lifts his chin in the direction of the kitchen where Memphis disappeared. "I think we both know that you've got an unusually strong interest in one of your employees. I don't need to know what the hell is going on to see that you're fuming, and because of that you're ready to piss all over your territory. Man, I'm telling you that you don't need to. I'm not trying to steal your girl. I've already got more women problems than I can handle as it is."

His startling accuracy has me leaning back in my chair to match his posture.

"I haven't heard a single word about you and a woman, so you're obviously better at keeping things under wraps than I am."

Bohannon's lips quirk up in a smile. "Grow up at the bottom of the food chain in Hollywood, and you learn a hell of a lot about how to keep shit quiet. You need any tips, I'm here." As if giving tips, unwarranted advice, and assistance is his hobby, he waits for me to respond.

I think of how I deliberately forced the idea of a relationship with Memphis to protect her from my father. "Too late for that."

Bohannon studies me as he takes a drink. "Something's not right. I have a feeling I know what it is, but given the situation, I think it's best we both let it lie for now."

Having a conversation like this, in the club, is bad for both of us, and he clearly knows it. But I would bet my Chevelle that he somehow has seen through Drew's disguise . . . which means things are even more perilous than I realized.

Who else knows? Who else will figure it out? Figure her *out?*

"You've been coming here a long time, Bohannon. I appreciate your discretion. Whatever you're concerned about, I've got it covered. You have my word."

I place my palms on the table and rise, but he stops me halfway.

"If anything happens to her, I won't let it go, Freeman. Understand me?"

Gripping the edge of the tabletop, I look him straight in the eye and give him what I know is the absolute truth, despite everything. "The only way something happens to her is over my dead body. That happens, feel free to step in and raise hell."

Despite the anger and betrayal simmering inside me, there's also a sliver of something urging me not to give up on Memphis. I may have inherited a newfound penchant for revenge from my father, but every other part of me that matters came courtesy of my mother and her soft heart.

Bohannon gives me a nod that carries the weight of his respect, and I walk away from the table in search of Memphis. She's not in the main area of the club or the kitchen, so I check the break room. She's just coming out of the ladies' room, and squeaks in shock when she sees me standing in the doorway.

"Jesus Christ, you scared the hell out of me."

I stare at her, with her ten pounds of makeup and colored contacts and wig, and I want to strip it all away. The restrictions that keep me from doing exactly what I want chafe like rusty chains.

"We're leaving after the midnight meeting. You're coming home with me. Understand?"

Her throat works as she swallows, and her eyes widen. But rather than protest, she nods slowly.

There are a dozen—hell, a hundred other things I want to say to her right now, but I promise myself I'll bide my time and get my answers. Every. Last. One.

"Keep up the good work, *Drew*."

CHAPTER
SEVEN

If it were news, I would report on today as the most awkwardly uncomfortable workday in the history of workdays.

Cannon stalks me like a predator after its prey. On more than one occasion, I catch myself vividly picturing the interrogation techniques he'll employ to get the truth out of me. *Or I just have a really active imagination when it comes to all things mob-related . . . and Cannon.*

Either way, I spend hours walking on eggshells and trying to be the very best server I can possibly be. Tanya calls to tell Letty they hit traffic on the way there and the rehab center needs her to stay for a mandatory intake family counseling session, so she and Warren won't make it back until after midnight. I don't envy Letty as she goes to deliver the message, but Tanya's decision not to call Cannon himself makes her more human to me.

I walk around the club like a live wire, jumpy and full of pent-up energy, serving bankers, CEOs, and a famous rapper turned producer. With each hour that passes, one would assume that my anxiety about being alone with Cannon would grow and grow, but it doesn't. *I'm ready.* I've been dying to come clean and get this burden off my shoulders, and I wish I could do it sooner rather than later.

Although, if I think about it, maybe it's a good thing he's had more time to calm down, because earlier today, I wasn't entirely certain I was going to be walking out of that construction site at all.

By the time midnight rolls around, all my nervous energy has burned off and I've given up on caffeine keeping me awake. I'm still upright due to sheer force of will. I just wish I'd been sharper, because then I would have gotten the hell out of the way when the Rossetti family contingent marched into the club after all the other guests had been politely ushered out.

"Damn, girl. That ass is *thick.*" The voice comes from behind me.

Startled, I spin around with greasy chills skittering down my spine. The leering dark eyes of the crown prince of the Rossetti family, GTR, lift to my face after pausing on my breasts for a solid count of three.

"Excuse me, do you need me to show you to the conclave for the meeting, sir?"

He sucks his teeth and rolls a toothpick to one side. "*Sir.* That sounds just right coming from you. What do you say you and me get out of here after, and I'll let you call me that somewhere more private?"

I paste a polite smile on my face as I extend my arm in the direction of the room where the meeting is taking place, but before I can say anything, a large source of heat appears at my side.

"Meeting's this way, GTR." Cannon growls the statement.

GTR is still leering at me with those dark, dead eyes when he replies. "I know where the meeting is, but I'm more worried about the entertainment."

Oh Lord. Now is not a good time for my stomach to roll, but as his nicotine breath wafts toward me, my insides revolt.

"If you don't want your head in a box to be the entertainment, then I suggest you move along. Now."

Finally, GTR jerks his attention to Cannon, his chest puffed out like a bull. "What the fuck did you just say to me? We're here to firm up terms of a truce, and you're threatening to put my head in a box? I don't fucking think so, asshole. This meeting ain't fucking happening. I'm out."

He steps back and turns around to smack directly into Dom.

Holy hell. All I want to do right now is *run.* But I stay still, invoking a combination of the three wise monkeys who see no, hear no, and speak no evil. In other words, I adopt all the qualities of a great fence post.

"You got a problem, GTR?"

As the head of the Casso family stares him down, GTR seems to actually shrink under the intensity of Dom's presence. "Uh. Well. You see—"

As he stutters out some gibberish, Dom stops him. *With a hard slap to the face.*

I jerk back in shock, my shoulder bumping into Cannon, and his hands land on my hips, as if keeping me safe and anchored to him. Given the volatile situation we're witnessing, I lean into his touch. That's twice today he's comforted me when he could have thrown me to the wolves.

GTR lifts his fingertips to his cheek in stunned silence as he stares at Dom.

"You ever run your mouth in my presence again, and I'll carve out your vile fucking tongue. You understand that, punk?"

I expect to hear GTR spewing vitriol and protests, but his sense of self-preservation must have kicked in because he does nothing but stand silently.

"That's what I thought." Dom claps his hands and replaces the menace on his face with a cocky smirk. "Your mother should have taught you better manners, boy. Go sit down before I have to tell your father what a piece of shit he raised."

GTR backs away from Dom with two steps and then turns to head to the conclave, but not before leveling a malevolent stare on Cannon and me.

Freaking fabulous.

CHAPTER EIGHT

The meeting didn't go well. The truce between the Rossettis and the Cassos lasted about as long as I expected, which wasn't long, and Dom is fucking pissed.

As soon as Dom's bodyguards and Grice escort the Rossetti contingent out of the Upper Ten, Dom looks at me and points to the door of the meeting room. "Shut it."

I rise and obey, waiting for his next order, because I know that this discussion isn't over. Lorenzo Angelini, who I'm still shocked had the intelligence to keep his mouth shut during the meeting, kicks back in his chair and puts his feet up on the antique table.

Clearly, Dom's number two's intelligence only lasted an hour.

Dom reaches out to smack him upside the head. "Sit right, you fucking idiot. You aren't five."

As Enzo practically falls out of his chair to comply, Dom points at me and then to the seat across from him.

"Take a seat. We need to discuss what the fuck

happened to blow all this shit up after I spent a goddamned year maneuvering Giancarlo into this."

"We all know what happened," Enzo says. "GTR. He ain't following Papa Rossetti's orders anymore."

When Dom's heavy gaze lands on Enzo, instead of waiting for Dom to speak, Enzo points toward the door and spouts off again. "Why don't you just give GTR the bitch he wants? I'm sure that'll get shit back on track, especially if he was willing to roofie her to get her."

As soon as the suggestion is out of his mouth, coupled with the information I gave Dom about the results of the test from Yoder, I want to vault over the table and beat him until he's sorry he ever uttered such horseshit. Instead, I curl my hands around the knobby ends of the arms of the chair and wait for Dom to explode.

He doesn't disappoint.

"You say one more word or do one more idiotic thing and I will slap you even harder than I hit the Rossetti punk. You want to pick up your teeth off the floor? Open your mouth again, Enzo." Dom loosens his black tie as if getting ready to do just that.

Apparently, the reign of Enzo's favoritism has ended. Still, I stay silent. It's one of the most important things I've learned over the last thirty years since I realized Dom was my father and not just a guy who visited my mom to take her on dates.

"That's what I thought," Dom says after a beat of silence. He leans back in the heavy wooden club chair, like a king holding court, and his attention swings to me. "What do you think we should do, Cannon?"

It's a test. Everything with Dom is a goddamned test.

After the day I've had, I'm fresh out of patience for his games, but I play along anyway out of necessity.

"How much money have you made in the last twenty-five years?" It's my best guess for how long the feud has lasted. It's probably closer to thirty years, to be honest, because my mother's death wasn't the beginning. No, she was targeted as a way to retaliate for something Dom had done to the Rossettis.

Dom blinks twice before reaching up to tap a finger to his lips. "A hell of a lot."

I lean on the armrest. "How much money would you have made if there'd been no feud with the Rossettis?"

His eyes narrow to slits. "Less. Competition is always good for business."

"Then other than the potential for less loss of life, which has dramatically decreased since the NYPD and the Feds are breathing down everyone's necks, what's the upside to ending the feud?"

Dom leans both elbows on the table and steeples his fingers. "You're saying we should forget trying for a truce and get back to business?"

Being that he sent me to one of the most prestigious business schools on the planet, Dom tends to listen to me when it comes to certain business matters, which is why I'm in charge of the Upper Ten. To my pride, it remains the crown jewel of his legitimate businesses.

"I'm saying that we don't let Rossettis disrespect us and then continue to offer them concessions."

A ghost of a smile hovers on Dom's lips. "You've got more of me in you than I thought."

It's the first time he's ever said anything like that in

front of another person. I'm partly shocked, but even more ready to bolt out of this room and get Memphis out of here, so I don't let any reaction show on my face.

Dom plants both hands on the table and pushes up to a half-standing, half-leaning position, and his gaze jerks between me and Enzo.

"Tomorrow, I send the message to the Rossettis that even the fucking idea of a truce is dead to us, with a nice little addition—I'll put GTR's head in a jar on my desk and use it for a paperweight if he pisses me off again." The hint of a smile curls into a full-blown wicked grin. "Prepare for war, boys."

CHAPTER NINE

CANNON

I find Memphis in the break room again, except instead of being startled when I enter, she's asleep in the chair in the corner.

"Come on, baby. Time to go."

Baby? Is that what she is to me, even after everything? And if not, why did it sound so right?

When she doesn't wake up, I shake my head, but rather than feeling annoyed, I can't help but think she's pretty fucking cute. Now all I can picture is her curled up in my bed, which is *not* how tonight was supposed to go.

Yes, I planned to bring her to my place.

Yes, I planned to interrogate her. But I didn't plan on wanting to see her hair splayed on the pillow next to mine when I woke up.

As I determined before, *I'm completely fucked.*

When she blinks her eyes open, the dark-colored contacts shift out of place for a second before sliding back to cover her aqua-blue eyes. After a moment of confusion, she jerks into an upright position.

"I'm so sorry. I—"

"It's fine. Let's go. It's been a long day." Without thinking about it, I hold out my hand, and I'm equally surprised when she takes it with no hesitation. There's so much that needs to be said between us, but the only question I truly care to have answered is the one I asked her at the construction site.

Was any of it real?

My instincts, which are rarely wrong after being honed through a lifetime focused on survival, say yes. It was fucking real. When I mentally rewind our every encounter, I see openings that someone truly opportunistic would have taken, but she didn't.

Maybe I'm grasping at straws here because I want to believe the narrative I'm spinning in my mind. Hell, there's no *maybe* about it. I am. But that doesn't make it any less possible.

Once she's on her feet, I grab her jacket off the chair and wrap it around her shoulders. "Come on, let's get out of here."

She glances up at me from under long dark lashes that at least I know are real. "Why are you being so nice to me?"

The question cuts me to the bone, and my jaw tightens. "We'll talk about it at my place."

Our ride there is silent. I still haven't had time to sweep the car for bugs, but I will in the morning.

"Why are you being so nice to me?" Her question repeats

in my brain as I park and open the door, but the only real sound is the grating metal of the overhead door closing us both inside my garage space.

When I unlock the entrance to the stark elevator lobby, the scent of pizza greets me. A puffy red delivery bag is sitting inside. *Geno.*

Of course. *Good man.*

Memphis's stomach growls as soon as the rich scent of tomato, basil, and melted cheese reaches her. "That man deserves a medal."

I crouch down to open the bag and remove the box, leaving the red delivery bag near the door Geno would have entered through. He'll pick it up in the morning, like he has so many other times before.

"He's a good one," I say.

We enter the elevator, and Memphis takes the box from me so I can close the gate and hit the button. It's a smooth, silent exchange, like we've done this together a million times.

This could be us . . . late dinners together after long days at work. Someone to smile with on the good days. And on the bad days, having someone to fight for *instead of* with.

The thoughts pop into my head, but I shove them down. *Not until I hear everything.*

With more silently choreographed moves, we enter my apartment, and I slide the pizza across the counter and grab two plates from the cupboard, along with a bottle of wine and two glasses. She waits for me to take a seat on one of the stools and I reach for the box, but instead of opening it, I rest my hand on top of the cardboard.

"I don't share my pizza with people who lie to me. For every bite, I want the truth."

Her form crumples and her elbows rest on either side of the plate, her hands catching her drooping head. "I'm so fucking sorry, Cannon."

She lifts her eyes to mine, and in them, I read anguish and guilt and myriad other emotions that send a shot of hope straight to my chest. Even if I can't see the real her beneath the makeup, contacts, and hair, her sincerity is as clear as the well-lit New York skyline outside my windows.

"I didn't mean for this to happen. I mean, that's not true. I did mean to deceive you. To lie to you. That's why I came. But I didn't mean to . . ." She trails off and sucks in a deep breath, like she's gathering her nerve.

"You didn't mean to what?" I ask before she can pull herself together. "To make me fall in love with you?"

I study her so damn closely that I see every tiny movement of her face, her hands, her lips, her chest. When she squeezes her eyes shut, the hope I feel dissipates a fraction more with each passing second.

But when she opens them again, shiny with tears, hope returns with a vengeance.

"I didn't mean to fall in love with *you*." She shakes her head, and the blond strands of her wig curtain her face until she brushes them away and meets my gaze. "But I couldn't help it."

She glances up at the ceiling again, like she can't handle the eye contact. "God, I'm so bad at this. I'm the one who asks the hard questions and hides behind my job. I don't get put on the spot or grilled or interrogated."

Everything she says makes perfect sense. Memphis Lockwood has a reputation for being a bulldog of a reporter, pushing and shoving her way through obstacles until she discovers the truth. But this woman, the one sitting two feet from me, isn't Memphis Lockwood. My gut says even if that is her real name, everything else about *that* persona is fake too. I'd bet this building on it.

I lean in, searching for the truth right in front of my face. "Which one is the real you? Any of them?"

With her lips pressed together in a tight line, she meets my gaze once more. "Every time I've been alone with you, I was more *me* than I've been in over a decade. And when I ditched the wig and the contacts and the makeup, I felt like I was stripping myself bare. I don't do that around anyone. Ever. Not even my own stepmother." She reaches out one hand and covers mine on top of the pizza box. "I know you have absolutely zero reason to believe me, but it's the truth. I didn't mean to show you the real me, but I couldn't help it."

Even though I believe every word, I can't let down my guard yet. Not until I've aired all my suspicions. "But you were hunting for evidence that you planned to turn over to the cops or the Feds to get me and Dom and the rest of the Cassos convicted of whatever you found so that we'd go down for your father's death."

"No." Memphis shakes her head, and her hand tightens on mine. "I would never have let that happen. I couldn't. At first, I thought I could, but then once I got to know you, I knew it was impossible. You couldn't have had anything to do with it. There's just no way."

"That's some pretty strong faith to have in another

person that you barely know," I say, considering her statement and wondering if I can make the same leap.

I have a choice to make, right here, right now.

I can believe her, take her words at face value—or I can hold tight to the feeling of distrust that's already slipping away from me. But I can't make this decision yet, as much as I want to.

Instead, I lift both our hands with the lid of the box, and the scent of the fresh-baked pie wafts out in a cloud of steam. "Eat before it gets cold."

Her gaze pins me, but she makes no move to take a slice. "I've never not solved a case. I've never walked away without an answer. Ever. I don't know how to leave something unfinished. But if you tell me that it's the only penance you'll accept, I'll try to find the strength to walk away from this. Either option leaves me with a broken heart, and I figure I've earned that for what I did."

My jaw tightens at the thought because I know first-hand what it's like to be in a situation that feels like you're drowning in lies without anyone there to throw you a lifeline. It's hell being caught between two conflicting worlds. I just hope I can figure out a way where she gets peace in hers and I still get to keep her in mine.

"Eat your pizza, Memphis. I didn't wait my whole damn life for a woman like you to come along just to break you."

CHAPTER TEN

What did he mean when he said he didn't want to break me? Are there any whole pieces of me even left under this mask I've been wearing for so long?

I'm totally lost and confused, and vulnerability wraps around me like a vise. What I said about not being in the hot seat or being forced to answer questions is the truth. I didn't realize by becoming an investigative journalist, I gave myself permission to stay guarded to the point where no one would ever see or know the real me.

Except this man.

I can't just bite into the pizza, regardless of how delicious it smells, without coming clean about one more thing.

As Cannon puts a slice on my plate, I blurt out, "I put a keystroke logger on the computer in your office here. Which you don't use, but you know that. I felt fucking horrible and guilty about it as soon as I did it, and if you want to turn me over to Dom and let him deal with me, I wouldn't blame you in the least." The weight of my betrayal lifts but doesn't go far—it only perches on my shoulders.

Cannon's hazel gaze sweeps over my face. "You're not a martyr. Don't get boring and start acting like one now." His words are like a twisted balm for my soul, because even with the sarcasm, they soothe me.

He's not going to hand me over to Dom.

All day, I've wondered, because he's had opportunity after opportunity. The torture of wondering and waiting was enough to make me resign myself to the fact that I'd let him choose my fate.

But Cannon's right. I'm not a martyr.

I lift the slice of pizza and we both eat in silence, watching each other before looking down or away. This awkwardness kills me, but I caused it. It's all because of me, and I have to make it right between us. Somehow.

Then an idea hits me.

"Do you want to see the file?"

Cannon's attention cuts to me. After he finishes chewing and swallowing, he asks, "What file?"

"My father was investigating the Casso family, like I told you. He had a file with photos dating back almost thirty years. I don't know where he got them or how long he'd been keeping it, but he was fixated on Dom and trying to take him down." I grab a napkin from the pile left from the other night and wipe my mouth.

"He could have tried, but nothing sticks to Teflon Dom. And Dom has never once mentioned his name, that I know of. I hate to tell you this, but I think you're looking in the wrong place." Cannon pulls another slice from the box and pops a few of the runaway toppings into his mouth.

"You really don't think it's possible?"

He shrugs and takes a huge bite, so I wait for him to chew and respond.

"Dom's capable of a lot of things, including murder, but I will say that he never does something without a reason. I don't have to agree with his methods to know that he lives by his own code of honor, as skewed as it may be."

I pour wine into both glasses and slide one to him. "Has he ever had a journalist killed?"

He nods his gratitude for the drink, slugs most of it back, and then answers. "I don't know. I spent a lot of years outside the family interests, keeping as far away from the business as possible."

"Why'd you come back?" I replace a crust with another slice on my plate and toss the doughy portion back into the cardboard box.

"Into the fold?" He leans back on his stool. It's the most relaxed he's looked all day. "Because of Enzo."

Like I'm seeing Cannon for the first time in a long while, I'm reminded of just how arresting he is. The earth, the forest, and the sky all live in his ever-changing eyes. Then there are the strong muscles in his jaw and the classic way his dark hair is swept to the side.

Before I get too caught up in the mere sight of this man, the one who has shifted so much of what I thought I knew about myself and my life, I shake my head and fight to focus and regain my composure. "Enzo? Why?"

Without skipping a beat, Cannon swipes my discarded

crust from the box, folds it, and eats it whole before he replies. "Dom considers him a potential successor. As much as I never wanted to be a mobster, there's no way in hell I can let Enzo take over. It'd be like letting a kid play with a fully automatic weapon after watching a decade of shoot-'em-up movies and thinking life is a fucking video game. It would be carnage. He wouldn't discriminate between guilty and innocent. He'd want blood in the streets as a way to cement his power."

A chill skitters down my spine as I picture dead bodies sprawled on the sidewalks of Hell's Kitchen. "Jesus Christ. What a disaster." Suddenly, my pizza doesn't seem so appetizing, and I put my half-eaten piece on his plate.

"And now we're at war with the Rossettis, and no one is safe."

The queasiness spreads to my stomach and arms, and I roughly brush my palms against the sleeves of my jacket, willing the goose bumps forming underneath to go away. "What are you going to do?"

He finishes my slice and closes the box. "Try to defuse it before anyone gets killed."

"How?"

"By taking out GTR and his dad."

I stare at the man in front of me—the man I could never imagine pulling a trigger on anyone, unless it was to save his own life or the life of someone he loved. *Will it come down to that?*

"That sounds dangerous as hell."

A smile flits over his lips, and for a moment, Cannon looks like a younger Dom Casso. "I may not be a mobster, but I know how to think like one." Quickly, he stands and puts the leftover pizza in the refrigerator, and when he turns back to me, his eyes are squinted and his mouth puckered. "Who knows, maybe Danger is my middle name."

The conversation should have been a deep, dark well of emotions and accusations. But it hasn't been—not even close. And there he is, making a joke to ease the tension that I brought to the table.

I smile, and he winks at me.

"Why are you telling me this? You shouldn't trust me with anything."

The brightest part of his smile dies, and Cannon's expression is freshly stamped with seriousness. "The other thing I know is how to trust my instincts. You're in love with me, whether it's as Drew Carson or Memphis Lockwood, and there's not a single fucking chance that you're going to betray me again."

He stalks around the island, and my chest rises and falls faster the closer he gets.

"You're my woman now, whether you like it or not." One corner of his mouth quirks up. "And I promise I'm going to make damn sure you fucking love it."

I stare at him in awe as he stops in front of me.

I excelled at hiding who I was from the world. Even more, I excelled at hiding my fears and my demons from myself. So, how in the hell did Cannon *Danger* Freeman find my heart anyway?

CHAPTER ELEVEN

I may not be a mobster, but I'm a man who knows what he wants and isn't afraid to take it.

Memphis is mine. For better or for worse. I'm claiming her and I'm not fucking giving her up, no matter what happens next. The decision is made, and the entire goddamned city could come at me and it wouldn't make a bit of difference. I'm not afraid of a challenge or to watch life unfold with uncertainty. Hell, I'm ready.

Bring it.

I sweep her off the stool, loving the expression on her face. That softness paired with amazement unnecessarily confirms everything I already knew. *It was all fucking real.* There's no doubt in my mind. She may try to hide behind her makeup and wigs, but I see through her now.

As I carry Memphis into the bedroom, the plan I have for our future is solidifying with each step. Whoever killed her father will face justice, and I'll help her make that happen—without getting her fucking killed.

I don't give a damn how she came into my life, only that she did, and I won't lose her now.

Once I've lowered her to her feet beside the bed, I place my palms on her shoulders and close the gap so that our faces are only inches apart.

"I'm in love with you, Memphis. From now on, it's just you and me. No more lies. No more hiding. Out in the world, you can be whoever you need to be and say whatever you need to say to keep yourself safe. But when it comes to *us*, there will be no more secrets."

Her eyes turn shiny again, and relief smooths her features.

Even as I make the proclamation, I know what I'm doing. I'm opening up the entirety of my past to her, along with my present, and most importantly, my future. *Our future.*

"You belong with me, and you're staying with me. We're a team, and we handle everything together. Got it?"

I never thought I'd say those words. Never thought I'd ever find someone who would understand my life, who could survive it along with me. With her beside me, I feel stronger than ever.

"It can't be that easy," she says.

A tear escapes her eye, and I lift my hand to catch it on my thumb. "Not everything in life has to be hard."

She presses her lips together and slips out of my grip. "Give me two seconds, okay?"

I let her move around me, and she disappears into the bathroom. The faucet turns on, and three minutes later, the real Memphis appears.

No wig. No contacts. Her face scrubbed clean of makeup.

"You're so fucking beautiful." I hold out my hand, and she crosses the room to take it.

"I'm in love with you too." The words tumble from her lips like she just realized how easy it was to say how she feels now that the disguise is gone. After a lifetime of hiding the real Memphis, she's letting me see *her*, and I'm fucking proud.

"Good, because this would be awkward as hell if you weren't." I lower my head and take her lips, catching whatever she was going to say next on my tongue.

The time for talking is later. Right now, I need to show her exactly what's on the table. We were fucking explosive together last time, and I know this time will be no different.

Her hands clutch my shoulders when I leave her mouth and trail my lips down her jaw, scraping my teeth along the tendons in her neck as her head falls back with a moan.

"So fucking beautiful," I whisper against her collarbone as I shove her club vest and shirt down her arms. Beneath is a silky tank I remove with ease, along with her bra. The skirt goes next, leaving her standing in front of me bare-faced and naked but for the tiny scrap of lace masquerading as panties. "On the bed, baby."

She backs up a step and bumps into the edge before sitting and moving into the middle. I slide my suit jacket over my shoulders and toss it on the chair behind me without turning to see if it made it. Memphis's gaze locks on my fingers, and I loosen my tie to slide it free. It follows my jacket. Then button by button, I undo my shirt. With each moment that passes, she shifts on the bed, her fingers gripping the coverlet, and I love it. I want her just as eager as I am.

I toss the shirt, then my belt, shoes, and pants. When I'm done, I stand before her naked, with my cock rising to bump against my lower abs.

Memphis sits up straighter as I place a knee on the bed and move toward her. Her hands outstretch, reaching for me, and I know I made the right decision.

Whatever else happens, I won't regret making this choice. I won't regret choosing her. Choosing us.

"You're mine," I whisper against her lips as I wrap my arms around her.

"And you're mine," she says. "I'm sorry—"

I nip at her bottom lip to stop her. "You apologized. I accepted. Now we move on. No more dirty little secrets, baby. Promise me."

Her forehead tilts to press against mine, and a shiver travels the length of her body. "I promise. How are you real? You should—"

Her head falls to the side as I grind into her center.

"Fuck you so hard that you have no choice but to fall asleep in my arms and not be able to sneak away in the morning? Yeah, that's my plan."

She goes quiet, reaching up to thread her fingers through my hair. "No matter what happens, I won't ever regret this, because I got to have you."

I don't like the fatalistic tone to her words, so I shut her up the best way possible—I kiss the hell out of her until she's pinned to the bed beneath me, and my hands rove freely. I memorize every curve of her body, every mole and scar and imperfection, because I want to know everything about her. Every detail, every story, every wrong turn she's ever made.

If I thought I was fucked before, I was wrong. *I was fucking blessed.*

With her moans in my ears and her nails digging into my shoulders, I make my way down between her legs and feast. Every tangy taste of her pussy fills me with resolve. When she screams out her orgasm, I don a condom and move into position. And for the very first time in my entire life, I don't fuck or bang.

It's *more.*

It's pushing and pulling together. It's this precious woman beginning where I end. It's passion and desire and lust and adoration. I give without taking, but gain anyway.

Slowly, I move inside her, savoring every quiver. Every pulse. Every moan. And for the first time in my life, I make love. It sounds cheesy as hell, but there's a goddamned difference, and I didn't know it until now. Until this woman.

For better or for worse, I'm never letting her go. Whatever happens next, happens to both of us.

And when I get closer, feeling the tension between us reaching a height I didn't realize was possible, her name pours from my lips.

"Memphis. Memphis. *Memphis.*" And I'm finally home.

CHAPTER TWELVE

MEMPHIS

From beside me, Cannon's breathing evens out as he drops off to sleep. I hover on the edge as well, my body sated and mind spinning.

How can he forgive me so easily?

There was only one man I knew who could do so with such ease, and that was my father.

He would have liked Cannon. I have no doubt about that. What he would have liked even more is the way Cannon treats his daughter.

As the garage door closed tonight, I was expecting rage and accusations. Outbursts and blame. But all I got was understanding and acceptance. Trust when I hadn't earned it. And through it all, he still wanted me, exactly as I am.

I already knew how I felt about Cannon before, but tonight cemented everything. *I love him, and there's absolutely nothing that could make me do anything to hurt him. Ever.*

I make the vow to myself, and I will die to keep it.

Whatever comes next, we will handle it together.

"I love you," I whisper into the darkness, and I swear his arm tightens around me. For the first time in months, I fall into a deep, dreamless sleep.

"I can't believe you didn't answer my calls, Memphis. I may not be your biological mother, but I'm the only one you've ever known."

Taking my mom out to dinner is pretty much the last thing I want to do right now, but I force myself to make a semi-sincere apology. "I'm sorry, Mother. I've been busy. I was undercover."

I don't know why I'm telling her the truth—or at least so much of it. I should lie to her, but lies don't come as easily to my lips today as they did before. And I know exactly why that is.

Because the truth feels damn good.

"You and your little investigations. Are you ever going to find a respectable hobby?" She lifts her third glass of wine to her lips and drains it, and we haven't even finished the escargot she insisted on ordering as an appetizer.

Since it's the only thing that makes them tolerable, I squeeze lemon onto the one and only snail I'll eat. Over-doing it on the citrus makes my lips pucker, but not more than my dinner date.

"It's not a hobby, Mother. It's my job."

She shakes her head, and her empty glass clinks against the plate as her hand trembles when she sets the crystal on the table. Clearly, Mother hasn't had enough to drink today to satisfy what her body has grown to need with her addiction.

"Oh, really? Is someone paying you to be undercover? Because Sandra Reddington told me last week at tennis that you took a sabbatical from the network, and Jim has finally given up hope that you're coming back."

It takes everything I have not to roll my eyes. Jim Reddington is a senior executive at Investigation Network, where I worked, and was a friend of my father's. He knew why I left, even if I didn't tell him, and he didn't try to confirm. When I rose from our meeting and shook his hand, he gave me a grave smile and said, *"Be safe and happy, Memphis. That's what your father would want for you."*

He offered to let me do the investigation as part of my role at the network, but when I declined, he didn't push the issue. Probably because he knew that this wasn't for public consumption, and I would never exploit what happened to my father for the sake of ratings. Besides, if I was right and my father died because he'd dug too deep into the dark recesses of the mob and paid the price with his life, nobody at the station would have been safe.

This is for *me* and the justice I need. I won't let a personal quest cost another life.

"Jim and I had an agreement, and what's more, it was a confidential one. Sandra shouldn't be saying anything about it."

The server keeps glancing in our direction but stays away from the table, like he'd rather not interact with my stepmother either. Smart guy.

My stepmother releases an exasperated sigh and maneuvers a snail off the serving dish and onto her plate with not-so-nimble grace. "Well, maybe I wouldn't have to go around asking for updates from my friends if you would answer your phone and tell me what's going on."

If I thought the woman across from me actually cared about anything I had to say, I might have told her more, but I've learned over the years that our interests don't overlap.

Maybe after all these years, it's time to search for relatives of my biological mother. My father told me she loved me dearly and passed away when I was four, and out of respect for Cynthia, he would prefer we not talk about her. While my instinct was to rebel against everything my stepmother told me, I followed my father's instructions like they came straight from the gospel.

I don't know why I didn't think more about her after . . . after what happened to my father. Probably because my sole focus in life since getting the call I never wanted to receive has been finding the truth and then gaining justice for him.

As my stepmother blathers on about her next snail being too rubbery or too salty, and *how can this possibly be a Michelin-starred restaurant with such terrible service because I finished my glass of wine three minutes ago and no one has come to refill it,* I zone out.

At least, I zone out until I overhear an unmistakable voice—Randi Brown's voice—from just beyond my stepmother, telling her date she's ready to get the hell out of here.

I stare over my stepmother's shoulder at Randi as her

gaze zeroes in on me and she stops in midstep. What feels like every drop of blood drains from my face as we make eye contact.

I'm wearing Memphis Lockwood reporter-on-the-air persona tonight. No one should recognize me as Drew, but the hair on the back of my neck lifts at the way Randi is staring. It's like she sees right through me.

And right next to her . . . is GTR Rossetti.

Oh Jesus Christ. Oh Jesus Christ. Please don't say anything, Randi. Please don't say anything.

"Why the fuck are you stopping?" GTR asks her, pushing Randi along to get her moving again.

Randi rips her gaze from mine and locks arms with GTR. "Because I'm waiting for you, bad boy. Come on."

Before I can duck my head and pray she didn't just recognize me, my stepmother turns around and snaps her fingers in the air, rudely summoning the server who finally dares to come two steps closer.

"I need a refill. Right now." She shakes her head and turns back to me. "Next time, Memphis, you're taking me somewhere *nice.*"

My name rings in the air in my stepmother's tone of eternal disappointment, and there's no way Randi can miss it. She does a double take, her eyes narrowed on me in a quick glance over her shoulder as she leaves the restaurant.

Fuck. Fuck. Fuck. I have to tell Cannon. *Now.*

While my stepmother places her order for a dish that's not even on the menu, I pull out my phone and tap out a quick text.

. . .

ME: I'm at L'Atelier and GTR and Randi were here together. Randi looked at me too hard as they were leaving. Like she recognized me. My mom used my real name in front of her. Help.

As I type the words, I realize that I'm *fucked*. What if Randi says something to GTR about thinking she saw someone who reminded her of me? How long could something like that possibly take to make its way back to Dom? And if it gets back to Dom . . .

I remember the icy feeling of terror that suffocated me at the construction site when I thought he was coming to kill me because he'd found out my real identity. It's rising in me now, and my fingers curl into my cloth napkin while I grip the phone tightly with the other hand.

My leg bounces to dispel the nervous energy.

My stepmother corrects the server about whatever.

My breathing quickens as, once again, a very real threat settles into the pit of my stomach.

I pray to God my cell buzzes with a response that tells me Cannon is coming to the rescue. He said we were in this together, and I hope he knows what to do.

Which is when I realize that I've never relied on a man other than my father to come to my rescue. That's big. Huge.

And I hope it doesn't cause us to end up dead.

Mommy Dearest taps her fork against my crystal wineglass, jolting me back to the moment. "Memphis? Are you going to order? We're waiting on you."

I lift the corners of my mouth into a fake smile that

I'm sick of wearing. I'm tired of hiding. Being in disguise. Not being able to show how I feel.

It's time for a change. It's time to just be me.

But a feeling of unease creeps up my neck.

"Still deciding. What do you recommend?" I ask, not bothering to look at the server. Instead, I glance over my shoulder and find GTR's gaze drilling into me. He and Randi hover near the exit, with GTR talking on his phone.

Fuck. Fuck. Fuck. Please be talking to your driver and not someone else. Like your father. About how you're going to bring something big to Dom to try to repair the truce.

My thoughts race as the server gives an effusive description of a fish I've never heard of nor care to eat, but I blurt out, "I'll have that. Sounds great."

My phone vibrates, and I don't even try to be polite. I lift it and stare at the message.

CANNON: I'm on my way. Stay strong, baby. We got this.

Baby. It's such a small word, but it packs a massive punch of feeling.

As I read the words, it's like being wrapped in a heated blanket. Warmth and concern cocoon me. While I don't know how Cannon plans to handle things so that we don't end up dead, I believe that he will. I have faith in him.

I glance at the door again to find Randi and GTR are gone. *Thank God.*

"Memphis? Are you even listening to me? Of course

you're not. Why would I expect that you'd care about a word I have to say after you've ignored my calls for weeks?"

Something snaps inside me as I fix my eyes on the face of the woman who wanted nothing to do with raising me.

"When's the last time you called me to find out how I was doing? You know, instead of just because you needed something. When was the last time you cared how my job was going? Or my life?" I toss my napkin atop my uneaten snail. "Or how I've been dealing with my grief? As a matter of fact, when was the last time you cared about something other than *yourself*?"

Apparently once the truth gates are open, anyone can get sucked into the undertow. At that moment, it's my mother, but sometimes the truth hurts.

I'll give credit to the Botox and fillers she's gotten, because her eyebrows don't move, although there's still a semblance of shock on her face.

"*How dare you* speak to me like that?" The outraged tone punches through every self-righteous word she speaks. "I am the closest thing you have to a mother, and you should be happy you have at least one parent left." Like she has to illustrate what a cliché she is, her jittery hand clutches her pearls.

The closest thing I have to a mother.

The words stick in my brain as a few patrons stare at the small scene we're making in this acclaimed restaurant, but I don't care if they watch. It's safer if people see me. Safer with more eyes on us, especially until Cannon gets here.

"You're right. But sometimes close isn't enough. You've

never wanted me in your life. You've resented me since I was old enough to know what resentment is. Why are you even here? Why did you even want to see me?"

A single tear tips over her lid, and a stab of sympathy pierces my chest.

"Because I don't have any family left either, Memphis. Did you think about that?" She shoves away from the table, the Hermes bracelets encircling both her wrists clinking against one another. Snatching up her vintage Louis Vuitton speedy bag, she stalks away to the restroom.

Instead of feeling vindicated and proud of myself for finally expressing my feelings, I feel like an asshole.

I guess it's no surprise why I've avoided having personal relationships for most of my life. The truth doesn't discriminate; it can hurt anyone.

The entrées are served and still my mother doesn't return. I stare down at the fish covered in a pungent truffle sauce and wait, thinking about one of the few times we actually got along. When I was eleven, she took me to Neiman's to go shopping for my first bra, and we ended up on a shopping spree. It was before the drinking got bad. *Maybe I should try harder to convince her to go to rehab.*

As I consider the idea, I realize how much time has passed when Cannon walks in the door of the restaurant. He waves off the maître d' and strides toward the linen-covered table.

Leaning down to press a kiss to my cheek, he whispers, "Where's the lioness?"

"I pissed her off and she ran to the bathroom." I glance

down at my phone to check the time. "Twenty minutes ago."

Cannon's eyebrows go up and he stands to his full height to help me out of my seat. "Why don't you go check on her. I'll take care of the bill."

"I can pay—" I reach for my bag.

"Memphis." He slips out a billfold from behind the lapel of his silk-lined jacket. "Go find your mother."

I follow his orders, but she's not in the restroom. I check every stall. When I come out, Cannon is standing near the door.

I wrap my arms around my waist and shrug. "She's gone."

"Fuck," he whispers.

"Ma'am?" an older gentleman says. "Are you looking for the blonde in blue Chanel who stalked out a little bit ago?"

Relief floods me. "Yes. Did you see her?"

"She said she was going for a smoke," the man says, then corrects himself. "A fucking smoke, actually."

I jerk my head back in shock. "A smoke? Thanks." Turning to Cannon, I add, "That's weird, because she doesn't smoke. Or at least I didn't know she smoked."

He threads his fingers through mine. "Come on, let's find her."

But when we make it to the sidewalk, there's no sign of her, and my apprehension grows with every minute that passes.

I ask the first thing that comes to mind. Although, I'm uncertain if I want the answer. "If Randi figured things out and she told GTR . . . he wouldn't tell Dom, would he?"

"No, I don't think he would."

Cannon leads me to a town car double-parked in front of the restaurant, and I pause as a driver I don't recognize opens the back door so I can climb in.

Cannon notices my hesitation and waves the driver off. "I've got it." Then he whispers in my ear. "Warren can't see you as Memphis. I've got you covered."

Another wave of wonderment at how capable Cannon is washes over me, and we slide inside. Once the car pulls out into traffic, he adds, "Call your mom. Maybe she just went back to the hotel." His arm slides around my shoulders.

Still holding my cell, I dial her number, but she doesn't answer. I shoot her a text.

ME: I'm sorry, Mom. I didn't mean to upset you at the restaurant. Can you please call me?

Thankfully, the reply is immediate.

MOM: I don't want to talk to you right now. Call me tomorrow and maybe I'll let you apologize.

I show the message to Cannon, and he reads it before glancing at my face.

"Does that sound like something she'd say?"

I scroll so he can see the previous texts, which include many variations of similar statements.

MOM: I'm too busy to talk. Call tomorrow.
MOM: Could you please choose a time more convenient to call me? It's too early. I'm going back to sleep.
MOM: Why haven't you called me like I told you to?

"Point taken," Cannon says as I slip my phone back into my purse. He reaches out to take my hand and squeezes it before pressing my knuckles to his lips. "I'm sorry dinner didn't go as you planned."

His kindness is almost enough to make me forget why I needed him there in the first place. "At least there was no sign of *them* on the way out. What are we going to do about that?" I try to speak in code, because even if Cannon's not worried about this driver seeing me as Memphis, I don't want to take any more chances by saying the wrong thing.

Cannon squeezes my hand again. "First, we're going to your mom's hotel and make sure she made it back safely."

Whatever my issues with my mom, the thought of her not making it back safely strikes a chord of fear in my chest. She's right. She's the only parent I've got left, and I absolutely do not want to lose her too, despite everything.

Cannon must read the concern on my face, because he resituates himself beside me so he can cup my cheek with his other hand. "Everything's fine. Stop borrowing trouble."

I nod and soak up the heat from his skin, wishing I could say all the things I'm thinking right now, and hating that we can't.

How has he managed to live like this? Always being on guard and knowing he has to watch every word that comes out of his mouth?

Oh, wait. That's exactly how I've been living for *years.*

But something has changed, and now the personas I used to slip on and off with ease all seem painfully restrictive. And I know exactly why.

Because Cannon saw the real me and accepted me for exactly who I am. Nothing more. Nothing less. No disguise. It was heady. No, more than that. Addictive. Freeing. And I want more of it, with him.

When we reach the Plaza, Cannon and I both climb out of the town car after the bellhop opens the door. At the desk inside, I give the attendant a polite smile.

"Hi, I'm Memphis Lockwood."

The woman's black eyebrows shoot up to her equally dark widow's peak. "I've seen you before. On TV." She jerks a look to either side, like she's afraid she's being watched. "I'm so sorry, but I can't give you any information for whatever you're investigating, ma'am. It's against policy."

"It's not official business, I promise . . ." I glance at her name tag. "Brianna. My mother is staying here. Cynthia Lockwood. We got separated on the way back from dinner, and I want to make sure she made it back safely.

She's not used to the city and her phone is dead, so I can't reach her."

"Your mother?" Brianna looks suspicious as hell, but to her credit, she types something into the computer.

"Yes, Cynthia Lockwood."

Given the fact that we have the same last name, I'm hoping Brianna breaks protocol and can give me something. She looks up from the computer and glances between me and Cannon.

"I'm not technically supposed to confirm or deny if a guest is registered at the hotel, and I can't give out room numbers. But if you give me a description of what she looks like, I can tell you if I've seen her come through the lobby recently."

Cannon curls an arm around my hip and squeezes.

"That'd be great," I reply, then give her a rundown of my mother's perfectly coiffed blond updo and the blue dress she was wearing tonight.

"I remember seeing her!" Brianna chirps brightly. "She stopped to request softer pillows and a minibar restock before going up."

"Thank you," I tell her with a smile as Cannon's grip tightens on my hip. "I really appreciate that."

As we leave the desk, I glance up at him. "I'm surprised you didn't try to slip her some cash to get her to talk."

One side of his mouth quirks up and there's a gleam in his gorgeous eyes. "Did you want me to?"

"No, but . . ." I reach for his hand and weave our fingers together.

"You're the most capable woman I've ever met. You had everything under control." We pause at the revolving glass door, and a burst of fresh air blows by with each new guest that enters through it. "But if you ever want me to jump in, all you have to do is give me a sign."

"I think I just fell in love with you all over again," I whisper just loud enough for him to hear over the voices in the lobby.

He pulls me tighter into his side and leans down to brush his lips against my cheek. "If that's all it takes, I'll have you falling in love with me all over again every damn day."

"Can we go back to your place now?" I ask, trying to keep my tone light, but really, I just want to climb him like a tree and show him exactly how I feel about what he just said.

"Damn right. That's where we're heading next."

But as I slide into my seat in the town car, my purse starts buzzing.

Jesus Christ, Mom. Your timing blows, I think as I fish it out.

But it's not my personal phone with my mom's number on the screen. It's Randi's number on my Drew Carson cell.

I flash it at Cannon as the driver pulls out into traffic. "What do I do?"

"Answer it."

With a swallow, I tap the screen and lift the phone to my ear. "Randi?"

"I don't know what the hell is going on with you, or why you looked different at the restaurant tonight, but you need to get home. Your apartment door is kicked in." Her voice, in true Randi fashion, is loud enough that

Cannon can hear her too. "I called the cops, but who knows how long they'll be."

"*Fuck*," he whispers and then rattles off my address to the driver. "Tell her we're on our way."

"I heard him," Randi says. "And you owe me a fucking explanation, Drew. Seriously."

CHAPTER THIRTEEN

CANNON

To her credit, Memphis doesn't ask the question, *"Who would break into my apartment?"* I think we're both well aware that her very existence is sending up red flags all over the city.

"It's going to be fine. I promise," I tell her as we pull up and she reaches for the door handle.

"I really, really hope you're right." She looks around, probably scanning for the cops that are supposed to be here, or at least on their way. But no one's here yet. Typical of the overburdened NYPD.

"You want me to come up, sir?" Yuri, the driver, asks from the front seat. I keep his number handy for random jobs like this.

"I'd appreciate it if you'd stay with the car. Direct the cops up when they arrive."

Yuri gives me a short nod, but I can tell from his posture that he doesn't like having anything to do with the cops. Given what I know about his past, it doesn't surprise me. Old habits die hard, or not at all.

Memphis retrieves her keys from her purse and hands them to me to unlock the first door. Then she pulls out her phone and taps at its screen.

"I have security cameras hidden," she says, lifting her chin at the lobby ceiling. "Here and near my apartment. We should be able to see something on the feed."

"Smart girl," I say, opening the door and ushering her inside.

She's still waiting for the camera feed to load due to the crappy service inside the stairwell when we reach her floor. Randi leans against the hall wall opposite Memphis's door, and the expression on her face can only be described as supremely pissed off.

"Good. You're here. See you later." She turns to stalk off down the hallway.

Memphis bolts forward to catch her. "Wait, Randi. I'm sorry."

Randi shoots a glance at me, and I can tell she wants to call Memphis out about what happened at the restaurant, but she doesn't.

Could she actually care about not blowing Memphis's cover, even though she's furious and knows she's been lied to? As if I'm one to talk. Only yesterday it was me getting gut-punched with the truth, and here I am. Memphis has that unique effect on people.

"Yeah, whatever. Good luck, *Drew*. Hope they didn't take anything important." Randi turns the corner and disappears, leaving Memphis with her phone in her hand, staring after her.

I move closer to the door to check out the damage to

the handle and locks. "Boot prints. A man kicked it in. Someone big or unusually strong for his size."

"I have dead bolts."

I glance her way for a beat before pulling down the cuff of my shirt to open the door without getting fingerprints on it. "If someone's determined, no dead bolt is going to stop them."

With a frustrated shake of her head, she looks back down at the phone and taps the screen several times. As I swing the door open, she looks up toward the position where I assume her other camera should be . . . and there's nothing.

Memphis meets my gaze, her mouth falling open. "How could they chance taking that camera out without being filmed? Wouldn't they have to know it was there?"

"Come on, let's check out the inside before the cops get here."

In the pit of my stomach, I know we're dealing with a professional. Even with the boot print and obvious signs of forced entry, which would make someone think this was an amateur job, I make a different conclusion. Someone wanted it to *look* amateur, which is even more telling.

"Holy shit." Memphis gasps when we walk into the living room. The entire place has been torn apart. *Ballsy as fuck*, given the fact that this apartment building could not have been empty when the break-in went down.

The couch cushions are slashed, erupting with stuffing. The drawers in the tables in front and beside the sofa are tossed on the oak floor, the limited contents spread out on the wood. The kitchen is the same. Every drawer and cupboard open. Food spilled everywhere. The fridge and freezer have been pawed through too.

Someone was looking for something specific. The only question is . . . *did they find it?*

Memphis charges toward what I assume is the bedroom, but I grab her hand. "Careful. I'm going first."

"But—" She cuts off what she was going to say.

Even rattled, she's braver than most men I know. Still, her safety is something I take seriously, even if she doesn't sense the danger.

"You going first isn't going to change anything. If they found what they were looking for, it's gone regardless."

"Fuck. Fuck. *Fuck.*" She curses but falls into step behind me.

The apartment's walls are bare, which goes along with the rest of the place, as it hardly looks lived in. I recognize a crash pad when I see one. Not that I expected this place to be Memphis's true home, and maybe that's a really fucking positive thing right now. Because she's just worried about what's missing rather than feeling violated by her space being broken into.

At least, I hope so.

I reach the bedroom, and it's a repeat of the kitchen. Every dresser drawer is open. Clothes all over the floor. Bedding and mattress slashed. Feathers from the pillows leave a dusting of white on top of it all. The walk-in closet is trashed, and so is the bathroom.

But thankfully, there's no sign of anyone.

Sirens wail in the distance, and I jerk around to look at Memphis. "Cops are coming. What were they looking for, and did they find it?"

She snatches up something from the mess on the floor and rushes to the bed to climb atop the ruined mattress. Using a metal fingernail file, she unscrews the vent cover above the bed and tosses it onto the pile of fluff.

"They didn't find it!" Triumph rings in her tone as she removes a file folder.

The sirens grow louder as I join her on the bed, taking the screws from her and replacing the vent cover as fast as I can.

"We're running out of time. Grab a bag. Bury the file, preferably in a hidden compartment if you have anything like that, and fill it with whatever clothes aren't trashed and whatever else you need. You're not staying here."

I offer her a hand to climb off the destroyed queen bed and tell her the plan. There's no room for fuckups, and we need to be on the same page.

"It'll take the cops hours to go through the place, but I want your shit out of here before they pull up. I'll run your bag down to the car through the side door, which is probably how they came in, if they knew about your camera in the entryway. I doubt we'll see a single face on your feed that'll help. But first, give your statement to the cops and call the building super. As soon as the door is secured and the cops are out of here, we're going to my place. Got it?"

Memphis nods and shoves the file at me. "Give me two minutes."

True to her word, I'm walking out of the apartment building three minutes later with a suitcase. Yuri stows it in the trunk just as a squad car pulls up.

CHAPTER FOURTEEN

MEMPHIS

I wait outside my apartment for Cannon to return, along with the cops, but something's nagging at me. After taking a few steps down the hall, I knock on Randi's door.

"Randi, can we just talk for thirty seconds before the cops get up here?"

I consider she might have left to avoid all the commotion, but then I hear her argue through the door.

"Why? So you can lie to me some more?"

"I'm sorry. I really am. I promise I had a good reason." Although I'll never tell her what it was.

Her door opens an inch, and the fastened chain blocks part of her face. "I thought we were friends, Drew. Or whoever you are. I don't even know your goddamned name. That's not how friendship works." She shakes her head, sending her silver-and-black hair flying. "I told you *everything* about me, and you just *lied.*"

"I know. I know."

Part of me wants to tell her why, but I'm not an idiot.

The company she's keeping means she can't be trusted with the truth under any circumstances. But still, I like Randi, and I don't want her to end up mixed up in something that's as bad as the Rossetti family.

So instead, I ask, "That guy in the restaurant, he was the same guy from the bar?"

Randi lifts her chin. "So what if he was? I can fuck the same guy more than once if I want."

"He's not a good guy, Randi. I know you might think he is, but he's dangerous. Please don't see him again." She doesn't have to accept my apology, but I pray she at least heeds my warning.

This knocks a guffaw from her throat. "Are you fucking kidding me right now? *He's* dangerous? Look at your own situation. Who did you roll up with?" She clucks her tongue, and her eyes shoot daggers over my head. "Oh, wait, that's right. You know exactly who he is because I told you everything I knew when you pumped me for information. Nice."

"I know you're pissed. But please, just listen to me."

Footsteps and men's voices echo from the stairwell as Randi shoves her door shut. I stop it with the palm of my hand.

"Please, Randi. Just be safe."

"Watch your own ass, Drew. Mine's covered." She shoves her weight against the door, and it slams shut.

Great. Awesome. Fabulous.

But I don't have time to think about Randi for much longer, because another familiar and completely unwelcome person follows Cannon to stand outside my door.

Detective Clinton Cole.

"Memphis Lockwood. How 'bout that?" He tilts his head to the side like he's taking in my appearance with leisure. "Just when I told myself I was looking for things where there was nothing to be found the other night, here you are with Cannon Freeman. Now, who's going to tell me what the fuck is going on?"

CHAPTER FIFTEEN

CANNON

Cole is the last person I expected to show up right behind the squad car, but sure enough, there he was.

"Can we talk about the break-in? Because as far as I'm concerned, that's the only thing that matters right now," I say, interrupting what I'm sure is about to be an interrogation from Cole about why Memphis has been hiding her identity.

The detective glances from her to me. "You don't want to talk about your employee's—or is it girlfriend's—multiple identities? Assuming you already knew about them, that is. Maybe I should take her into protective custody, just in case you have any thought of doing her harm now that you've found out she isn't who she said she was."

Where Cole is getting all this, I don't know, but I suppose I shouldn't underestimate the NYPD detective so easily. But one thing is absolutely certain—he's not taking Memphis any fucking place.

"I'm safe, Detective," Memphis says, crossing the hallway to stand at my side. "In fact, there's nowhere I could possibly be safer than with Mr. Freeman."

The detective is skeptical and studies our united front before waving the patrolman toward the door. "Don't fuck up anything. Crime scene unit is still on its way to get fingerprints, photos, and to collect evidence." He pauses to look back at us. "At least you were smart enough not to go inside."

"Actually, we did," I tell him. Mostly because I know our footprints and fingerprints will be found if they're thorough.

"Of course you fucking did," Cole says. "Why would you bother with common sense when you think you own the world? While we're on the subject, did Dom have anything to do with this? You know I'd love another piece of evidence to throw at the DA so he can try for another conviction."

Why the man lets it all hang out when it has to make his objectives harder to attain, I have no idea. Does he actually think I'd implicate a single member of the Casso crew, let alone the head of the family? Either way, I give him a slice of the truth.

"No. Dom didn't have shit to do with this. We got a call from a neighbor while we were on our way home from dinner. We came back to find the entire place trashed. Seems random to me."

"Right," Cole drawls, sarcasm rich in his tone. Then his attention zeroes in on Memphis. "What are you investigating, Ms. Lockwood?"

"You know I can't discuss that, Detective. But I think Cannon's right. The break-in seems totally random."

Cole eyes her as his jaw tenses. "Secrets don't make friends, Memphis. We could help each other out. You have to have some idea of what they were looking for."

I don't like his smooth tone, the one he probably pulls out to get way more information than people want to give. Maybe that's how he gets his real work done. But thankfully, my girl's too smart to bite.

"I don't know. The place was too much of a mess to tell if anything was taken."

"Laptop?"

She curses softly. "*Shit.* I didn't even look." Memphis sounds genuine enough to me that I wish I'd thought to look for one.

Cole narrows his gaze on her. "Then what were you looking for when you went inside?" He scans her form, pausing when his gaze lands on her purse. "If you removed anything from the crime scene, I'm going to need to know about it."

"Do you see her carrying anything, Cole? Because she's not. And correct me if I'm wrong, but isn't she the victim here? You mind easing up on the accusations?"

Cole shoots me a sideways glance that tells me he believes me about as far as he could throw me, but without proof, it doesn't matter. Besides, it's not like Memphis could ever be prosecuted for taking something of hers out of her own apartment. Cole's fishing, and he's canny enough to snag a piece of information here and there with his technique.

Memphis watches the uniformed officers file in and out of her ransacked apartment and then turns on the charm I've seen her use with patrons at the club. "I'd really like to go back in and check for my laptop, Detective. Along with that, I should be calling my super to get someone up here to secure the door. You don't mind, do you?" She smiles, but it's fake, and I like that she gives me the real ones. "It's been a long day."

God, she's good.

Finally, the cop relents and lets Memphis and me back into the apartment. Thankfully, her laptop is still there.

Three hours later, crime scene techs leave with finger-prints, the boot print, and photos of the wreckage. Cole stays through every single moment of it, which doesn't make any sense. The man's got plenty of better shit to do, and I don't know if it's my presence that's attracting his attention or if it's Memphis. Either way, we're going to have to figure out what his angle is.

The super secures the apartment and gives Memphis a new set of keys.

We take another small bag of her salvageable clothes and toiletries with us when we leave, and Cole follows us out to the curb.

"I made a call after I thought I recognized you before, and I was surprised to find out you're not at Investigation Network anymore. They said you'd taken a leave of absence for personal reasons."

Memphis takes a deep breath before she finally replies. "My father passed away."

Instinctively, I wrap my arm around her side.

"And you're investigating his death." Cole's words are a statement, not a question.

Memphis doesn't flinch, but her tone is defensive. "His death was ruled a suicide, Detective, so why would I be investigating it?"

"I made some calls about that too. Detective on file said you didn't believe the injury was self-inflicted and swore you'd find the truth." Cole shifts his weight and crosses his arms to scrutinize the woman beside me. "So, you're telling me you left the network to *grieve* in this apartment that's a shithole compared to your father's place in the Upper East Side? Doesn't make a hell of a lot of sense to me."

To her credit, Memphis's posture and body language don't change at all. In fact, she doesn't even respond.

I'm finished with the whole situation and ready to get home where we can finally breathe after the day from hell. "Are you trying to make a fucking point, Detective?"

Memphis finds her voice again and adds without missing a beat, "I think he's just being an asshole."

Cole has the audacity to laugh and shoots me a grin. "You've got yourself a smart and sassy one, Freeman. I hope you know what to do with her."

Before I open my mouth to reply, Memphis beats me to it.

"Save your misogynistic bullshit, Cole. My apartment was just torn to shreds, and I'd like to go get a good night's sleep so I can figure out why. I'll consider updating you when I figure it out before you do. It wouldn't be the first time I helped the NYPD do their job."

Cole's grin fades, and I give him a hard stare. "I guess we'll be in touch then, Cole."

But as we walk away, I know it'll be a cold day in hell before I contact any cop—especially Clinton Cole—to swap intel.

That's not how shit works in the Casso world.

CHAPTER SIXTEEN

MEMPHIS

The ride back to Little Italy is quiet, mostly because I'm uncertain if it's safe to speak freely in front of the driver, despite Cannon's earlier comment about having everything covered. But as soon as we haul both my suitcases up to his apartment and the door shuts behind us, I ask him, "What the hell is the deal with Clinton Cole? Is he really trying to bring down Dom? And does he have a death wish just telling you about it?"

Cannon carries the bags into his bedroom and flips on the lights. I follow him inside and plop down on the bed to open the suitcase that has the file inside.

"I'm not sure who else is paying Cole, but it's safe to guess it's not just the NYPD." Cannon tugs his neck in the opposite direction of the knot in his silk tie as he loosens it before pulling it over his head.

My eyes widen and my fingers slide across the manila folder. "You think he's dirty?"

His hearty laugh booms through the room. "You can't be surprised by that."

"The first time I met Cole was through NYPD internal affairs during an investigation into an officer-involved shooting," I tell Cannon for background. "So, yes, it actually does surprise me. A lot. I wouldn't have figured an IA cop would end up dirty."

Cannon's lips curl into a lopsided smile. "Because no one has ever let a fox guard the henhouse . . ."

"Touché." Gripping the file with both hands, I settle it onto my lap. "Do you want to see why I'm here?"

Cannon's gaze locks on what I'm holding. "Absolutely, but I have a feeling this is going to require food, which you didn't get a chance to eat, and probably booze. Am I right?"

Knowing what's inside the file, and especially what it will mean to him, I nod. "Well, *Danger*, now that you mention it, I wouldn't turn down some manicotti and a glass of wine."

He winks at my calling him by his silly, and totally bullshit, self-declared middle name, and straightens with his hands on his hips like a superhero. How can one man be so strong and powerful, and yet still playful enough to make all the crazy disappear—if only for a second?

His eyes still shining, he says, "I'll call Geno and get us set up. Use the coffee table in the living room so you have more space to spread it all out." On the way out of his room, he casually kisses my neck as I stretch, knowing it's going to be another long night digging through skeleton-filled closets.

While Cannon runs downstairs to get the manicotti, I

sit on the sofa in front of the square coffee table and open the file. Picture after picture of Dom Casso greet me, but my reaction to them has changed. Seeing Dom's face used to fill me with hate and vengeance because it reminded me of loss and pain, but now it's different. Now his face reminds me of someone I love.

When Cannon returns with the food, he sets it on the counter and waves me over to get some. While I go to town serving myself from the oversized container of delicious ricotta-filled pasta, he stands over the coffee table and stares down at the pictures.

"Jesus Christ. No wonder you had no choice but to find out why the hell your dad had all these pictures." He glances over his shoulder at me before turning back to point at one I can't see from where I'm standing. "These go back to when I was a kid. He had to have gotten them from FBI files and who knows where else."

Cannon picks up a picture, and I snatch up a napkin and bring my plate with me as I come closer to see which one he's looking at.

I chew and swallow a mouthful, surprised at how hungry I was. "I never could figure out who that guy was. There was only that one picture of him and Dom."

"Benny Romano. He retired and moved to Boca."

Cannon sounds like he knows Benny well. I feel a little awkward, not sure if I should be asking questions about these guys, and if I do, whether he'll even answer. But Cannon keeps talking without needing to be prompted, and I finish the rest of my plate.

"Believe it or not, he babysat me when my mom went

out on the town with Dom. You'll meet him at Dom's birthday party."

"Dom's what?" The mention of a party throws me off for a second.

"You're going with me, so don't argue."

I'm wise enough to pick my battles, so I drop it and ask about the harmless-looking older man I hadn't been able to identify before. "Was he one of Dom's main guys?"

Cannon's chiseled jaw cuts to me. "What are you going to do with the information I give you? Because I'm going to tell you right now that I'm not going to help you take down a single member of the Casso organization unless you have undeniable evidence they were involved with your father's death."

I press my lips together and try to figure out the answer to that question. "You're really sure Dom had nothing to do with it?"

"One hundred percent." His deep voice is resolute and sure.

"And no one else in the Casso family?"

"All I can tell you is that I can't think of a single reason why Dom or anyone under him would've given a single thought to a retired reporter, even if he was snooping around or making a scrapbook of Dom's life. You have to remember that no DA has ever been able to get a conviction on Dom."

My stomach twists because that's not the response I wanted. "I need to know for sure, Cannon."

He jerks away from me, his gaze turning hard, like when he was still a stranger to me, as it drills into mine. "So you what? Want to go ask Dom to tell you either way?

You think that's a good fucking idea?" Cannon's defensive, but even if he's had issues with Dom his whole life, Dom's still his family and that will never change.

"How else am I ever going to know the truth? *I need to know what really happened.*"

After the last few days of constant stress, the bullshit with my mother, my disguise coming off, and then my apartment getting broken into, I'm losing my ability to keep it together and think rationally. Usually I can compartmentalize, but there are so many things up in the air, so many pieces in play. And for once, I can't lock myself down.

Why did I think showing him this file was a good idea? That he would actually tell me anything? Stupid, Memphis. Stupid.

My hands trembling, I scramble to gather the photos and shove them back in the file, shifting into fight-or-flight mode and choosing flight because I feel like I'm about to *break* and that's not something I want anyone to witness. Not even the man I'm in love with.

I just have to hold it together until I'm out of his sight.

"What? Now you don't want to look at them because I'm not going to spill info that you can take to the cops? Info that could take down people I care about—people who may not have done a damn thing to you or your father?"

"I just . . . I can't . . ." I'm stammering with my back to him, praying he won't see how badly I'm clutching at my shredding self-possession. Even my mantra can't touch this.

"You got a better idea of how to deal with this? You think you're going to figure it out without me?"

With my stockpile of photos, articles, and notes, I rush to the counter where my purse is waiting and grab it. I don't know what else to do.

An insidious whisper enters my brain. *Maybe this was all a mistake. It couldn't be as easy as he claimed. Nothing ever is.* I don't want to believe that, though. I can't believe it.

Still, somehow, I shore up my poise and lift my chin high. "I can't do this with you right now." I don't bother turning around when I speak. If I do, I might not be able to walk away from him so I can break down in private.

I stride to the apartment door but Cannon is right behind me. He slams his hand on the steel panel, stopping me from opening it before my fingers grip the handle.

"Where the hell do you think you're going?"

A tremor rips through my body. *I have to get out. He can't see me break.* The thought repeats over and over in my head, and my mouth runs off without taking any cues from my brain.

"I don't know. But I can't sit here knowing that the answer to what happened to my father could be in this file, and you're staring at the pictures and won't tell me what I need to know!"

God, now I sound like a fucking bitch. But I can't rein it in.

Over the past few days I've had to make so many split-second decisions, and now I'm wondering how many of them were wrong. Even more, I'm wondering what price I'll have to pay to fix them.

"Would you let me explain? You're so goddamned stubborn," he says, his breath wafting past my ear.

Another part of me, the *big* part that wants to be as

close to him as possible, tells me to lean back. Press into his body. Let his strong arms wrap around me so that instead of seeing me break, he can hold me together.

"What? What could there possibly be to explain?" My voice threatens to crack, and the two warring factions inside me are threatening to tear me in half.

I know I offered to let go of my search for answers before, when the guilt of lying to him about my identity came out. *And I meant it.* But he also said he'd help me. *Did he mean that?*

Before the uncertainty takes me to my knees, Cannon grips my shoulders and spins me around to face him.

"Hey!" I screech in protest, but Cannon locks me in the circle of his arms, preventing me from doing anything but staring up into the burning heat of his hazel eyes.

"Do you really think the only reason I give a fuck about what happens with the photos in that file is to prevent you from finding out what happened to your father? No. Memphis, I'm trying to fucking protect *you*. I will lose my goddamned mind if something . . ." He draws a deep breath, bites his lip as if he's enduring a tremendous amount of pain, and the intensity in his face is wild. "I'm *never* going to let anything fucking happen to you. Period."

Cannon's words, filled with such emotion, hit me harder than the instinct to run and hide ever could. They shake me loose of the skeletal grip of my fear, and my shaking subsides.

Because he loves me.

And I love him, and I almost ran out on him the first time things between us got the least bit rocky.

That's not me. That's not how I'm built. I take a slow, deep breath, and my purse hits the floor with a thump. The file follows it.

When I throw my arms around his neck, the anguish on Cannon's face fades and the heat in his eyes burns in a new way.

Good. Because he deserves better than what I almost did.

"I'm so sorry. I just—"

He brushes his lips across mine, silencing the rest of my apology before I can get it out. "Baby, there's nothing I wouldn't do to protect you. Just fucking let me." His forehead lowers to mine. "Not even you can stop me."

The hands that were trapping me against the door spear into my hair as his lips crush against mine, taking my mouth and conquering all.

All the fear.

All the worry.

And every damn last scrap of control I thought I had.

CHAPTER SEVENTEEN

She's the most maddening woman I've ever met in my life, but she's all fucking mine and I'll never let her go. Memphis wraps her leg around my hip, locking our bodies together as I take the kiss deeper, desperate for the taste of her on my tongue.

I'm not going to lose her.

Getting the text from her at the restaurant, and rushing there as fast as I could to make sure GTR couldn't touch her, got my adrenaline pumping. As I relive the memory, it all dumps back into my system. The urgency to protect this woman was so visceral, so reminiscent of how I always wished I could have been there for my mother. I won't fail my girl the way Dom failed my mom.

Memphis's fingers attack my belt, ripping it loose before yanking down my zipper. As soon as my cock is free, I lift her higher and slide my palms up her legs and under her skirt, snapping the elastic of her panties and finding her soaked.

"Jesus, baby. You're already wet," I murmur into her ear as I slide a finger inside.

Memphis's moan fills the room as I pump my finger in and out, teasing her clit with my thumb and loving how her inner muscles tighten every time I hit the right spot.

And just like that, she's ready to go.

"Please, hurry. I want—"

"I know what you want, and I'm the only fucking man who's going to give it to you. Wherever I want. Whenever." I stare down into her blazing aqua eyes as moisture soaks my hand. "You like that."

Challenge lights up her face. "Seriously, what I need most right now is you inside me. Hurry up and fuck me."

A smile tugs at the edges of my mouth from her bossy words. "You're going to get everything you need. Right fucking now."

I lift her other leg to wrap around my hips, and using the door to brace her ass, I slowly lower Memphis onto my cock. Inch by goddamned perfect inch, I slide inside her tight, wet heat. *Fucking perfection.*

Her nails dig into my shoulders.

"Hold on tight, because this is going to get rough."

Memphis's teeth dig into her bottom lip, and I circle her waist with my hands and lift her up only to slam her back down on my cock. Over and over, until her cries and moans and whimpers bounce off the walls.

My orgasm is already tightening up my balls, and when Memphis screams my name, I can't hold back any longer.

"Fuck me, Cannon."

And I explode into her with a strangled yell.

Which is when I realize . . . we didn't use a condom.

Well, hell.

Our chests heaving and foreheads damp with sweat, we stare at each other. She must have realized the exact same thing because her color fades.

"I'm sorry. I should've grabbed a—"

Memphis interrupts, saying, "It's my fault."

"It's not. But I'm clean. I promise."

"Me too. And for the record, on birth control. We should be fine."

But I already know that too. Not the fact that she's on birth control, but that we'll be fine. No matter what happens, I would never not be a part of my kid's life—or their mother's. My mom raised me better than that.

"I know. Everything will be okay." I lean down to press my lips against her forehead. "But it's going to get a little messy for a second. You ready?"

Memphis nods and uncurls her legs from around me, and I lift her so she can find her footing.

I grab my pocket square, more decorative than functional, and hand it to her so she can clean herself up. Then I crouch down to grab her purse and the file, including the pictures that scattered all over my floor. I hate that her first instinct was to run, but I know that the shit she's been dealing with is heavy. Whether she expects it or not, I'm here to lighten her load.

"No running. We're going to talk about this because we need to get a few things straight."

With her lips pressed together, she nods, and I move back to the couch.

I drop the file on the coffee table and wait for her

while she ducks into the bathroom to clean up. When she reemerges, she crosses the room to stand a few feet away from me, and it's too fucking far. I want her closer. I *always* want her closer.

"Come here." I pat the seat beside me on the leather sofa.

Although I'm sure she hates being told what to do, she obliges without hesitation. I'll do damn near anything to make sure she always knows she can come to me.

However, there's still one thing we need to clear up when it comes to getting her vengeance.

"I'll help you find whoever took out your father, but you're going to promise me that we make the decision together as to what we do with that information."

Her lips press together, and she stays quiet for a solid thirty seconds before replying. "Okay. But what if you're wrong and Dom did it . . ."

"He didn't. He hasn't pulled a trigger or done wet work in over a decade, Memphis." To her credit, and probably due to her research and investigations, she doesn't ask what wet work is.

A single eyebrow raises, and she tilts her head. "But if he gave the order—"

"Let's find out what the evidence shows first, and then we'll go from there." I push a stray lock of her dark hair over her shoulder. "If I told you right now that I'll put him away no matter what we find, you'd know I was full of shit. Right?"

She inclines her chin, and I keep going.

"But I'm not full of shit. I've lived on the edge my whole life. The edge of crime. The edge of respectability. I know how to walk that line between two worlds, and that's exactly what I'm going to do with you. Let me be your guide to this shit. Because I swear to God, I won't let you risk yourself by rushing to Dom right now, demanding to know if he had anything to do with it."

Looking for any way I can to ease her stress, I slide my hand to the back of her neck and knead her muscles. Her eyelids flutter for a second, and her body relaxes enough to confirm it was the right move.

"But what are you going to do if we find out he gave the order?" Her voice is strong, although her eyes are becoming hazy from my movements.

I'm glad she's not cowed by me, because that's the opposite of what I want. I want her to have every goddamned thing she wants, but only if we can do it safely. Her head rolls when I add a second hand and massage her collarbone and upper arms as we sit face-to-face.

"Then we'll go to Dom, and I'll give him an ultimatum."

One curious eye peeks open. "What kind of ultimatum?"

"He turns over the name of the man who pulled the trigger, and that man will face justice one way or another. Then Dom steps down and retires."

"Or else what?"

"Baby, the mob doesn't give you options. If we make a move on Dom, that's his *only* option."

Memphis's shoulders jerk back. "And you think he'll go with it? Retire and turn over a name that we can hand to the DA? And whoever pulled the trigger goes to prison?"

Memphis only retreated a few inches, but I pull her back and continue working on her knotted muscles. "Let's go through the evidence first. We'll answer all those questions once we know exactly what we're working with." I give her a jostle to make sure she's really listening and add, "And no more fucking running away."

She bites down on her lip for a beat before replying. "I shouldn't have done that. I . . . It's been a lot lately. I . . ."

When she trails off, I clasp her hand between both of mine.

"You what?"

Her whole body shudders before she replies. "I lost the battle between fight or flight." Her gaze drops to her lap. "I didn't want you to see me break. It's not something I'd want anyone to see."

I swear to Christ my heart clenches, and I can't help it —I haul her into my lap and tilt her chin up to meet my eyes.

"I can handle anything you throw at me. *Anything.* If you think you're gonna break, you tell me, and I'll hold you together. That's what this is. You and me. The real thing." A tear tilts over her lid, and I sweep it away with my thumb. "I can even handle your tears."

I place a kiss on her lips and soak up the moment. Holding her against me. Feeling her heat. Knowing she's mine.

Against my shoulder, she whispers, "You're better to me than I deserve. Thank you."

I pull back so I can meet her gaze once more. "No.

This is exactly what you deserve. I'm on your team. I got you. Now, let's look at the pictures and see what we can figure out so we can put this to rest and move on with both our lives. Deal?"

A ghost of a smile tilts her lips. "Deal."

I seal it with another kiss, and in a matter of minutes, the coffee table is hardly visible as I rifle through the stack.

"Your dad had quite the interest in Dom. I'll definitely give you that." There are dozens of photos just of him. I lay them out in a line to my left. Dom getting in and out of cars. Dom in public places. At restaurants. His wife's funeral.

"You can see why my suspicions brought me here," Memphis says, looking sideways at me before glancing back at the table.

"Absolutely. But did you notice that the camera angle and style is always the same? Like the same photographer took a lot of these pictures?"

Memphis scoots closer to me and I lean in closer, catching the scent of her skin.

"Wait. You're right." She shifts to meet my gaze. "I always thought my father had cobbled together pictures of Dom from whatever source he could find, but—" She picks up the next photo on the stack, one of Dom walking into a restaurant, and then the one of Benny Romano on a street corner. "These were totally taken by the same person. What does that mean?"

The age of the photos is what has me wondering. Over half of them were taken over twenty years ago, and then there are some outliers that look like they were added within the last few years. "Could your father have inherited the file from someone? Picked it up off a friend who left it to him? A lot of these photos are really dated."

Leaning into my side, she reaches for another black-and-white print as the knuckles of her left hand turn white from squeezing it so tight. "Where did you get these, Dad?"

I cover it with mine, brushing my thumb over her strained hand. "I know you wish you could ask him, but I promise, we will find out the answer."

She groans, releasing her frustration. "You're right." And then she forges on.

One by one, we look at every single print. I give her location information, confirm the names of guys I recognize, and correct a few she got wrong. We make a pile of the pictures that caught a side profile of someone or something we can't identify.

"Do you care if I take pictures of these? I have an idea who we could ask for some help. Maybe get some context and answers."

Memphis turns, her knees bumping into mine as she surveys me. Even though the question should seem innocuous, I know it's much bigger.

It's a test. *Do you trust me?*

Sooner than I expect, she asks, "Can you do it safely?"

"I would never put you at risk."

Her brows dart together. "Not me. *You.* I don't want to put *you* in danger, Cannon."

Everything that's been growing and forming inside me furls open. I lift a hand to her face to sweep my thumb across her cheek. It is dangerous, but I love her.

She's worth the risk. Worth everything.

"What did I tell you about *danger*, baby?" When I wink, she remembers, and I love how some of the worry in her face disappears.

Playfully, she rolls her eyes. "Oh yeah, it's your middle name."

"That's right. Besides, whatever happens next, I swear I won't let anything happen to either of us. Call me selfish if you want, but I need a hell of a lot more time with you. It's going to take a lifetime for me to peel back all your juicy . . ." I place a wet kiss at the crook of her neck, and she squeals. "Sexy." A *hmm* gets her another kiss. "Mouthy."

"*Hey!*"

I chuckle but finish my point. ". . . beautiful layers."

Her eyes meet mine, and the love there is stunning. "I want more time too, Cannon. A lot more."

Even though the next week is a madhouse at the club, and we're still waiting to hear back from the police about the break-in, Memphis and I somehow settle into a routine.

Work. Sex. Italian food. Research. Dead end.

I can't complain about business being good, but it only leaves us with scraps of time here and there, and we're not finding anything new.

On the other hand, the sex is fucking magic. She's as hungry for me as I am for her.

Every night it's new. On the counter in the kitchen. In the shower. In the back seat of my Chevelle parked in the garage—and I can attest to the fact that that's what my car was really made for.

Memphis Lockwood, the sable-haired, turquoise-eyed bombshell, has barreled into my world, and for the first time since my mother's murder and my falling-out with Creighton, I have a semblance of peace despite the amplifying tension between us and the Rossettis.

Something is in the air, and war is coming.

For now, I stare up at the ceiling and run my thumb up and down my woman's arm, push the dread aside for another night, and just focus on how fucking gorgeous she looked when she listened to her friend Ariel gush about her new baby over the phone.

With that image on a loop in my mind, I fall asleep to fight another day.

CHAPTER EIGHTEEN

MEMPHIS

"*S*alud, chindon!*"*

A drink is shoved into my hand as soon as I walk in the door. Even though we arrived on time, apparently we're late, and people are already toasting to Dom's continued good health.

When Cannon said he had an idea of who we could ask to get some more information, I didn't expect it to coincide with our attending Dominic Casso's seventieth birthday party, which is being held in an Italian restaurant that might as well be straight out of *The Godfather*.

The room is full of people I don't recognize, but I quell the urge to adjust my wig. I'm firmly in the role of Drew Carson tonight, even though being in disguise grates. All I want is to be *me*. Whoever that is.

But with Dom being such a big part of Cannon's life, I don't know if I'll get to shed my disguise anytime soon. Especially if people are toasting Dom another hundred years of good health.

Wait. Why do I know what that toast means in Italian? I

don't speak Italian. Obviously, everyone knows what *salud* means, but I must have picked up the other word somewhere along my career through osmosis or something.

I lose my chance to think about it any longer as Cannon is engulfed by the crowd. Men and women come forward to hug him, kissing both cheeks, and I wonder if they're straight from Italy or really just that effusive in their greetings.

Cannon introduces me to everyone as Drew, and I file their names away as they come at me. *Gina. Anthony. Rudy. Elisa.*

I sip the drink in my hand—a Bellini, I believe—as I smile, shake hands, and make small talk with people who come from a completely different world from the one I know. A world I planned to tear down to its very foundation.

Planned? As in past tense? I question my own thoughts as I scan the crowd for any familiar faces.

One pops up right next to me, but there's no smile on her face.

"He really brought you here? Wow. That's quite the statement," Tanya says with a wry smirk. It's hard to tell if she's friend or foe.

"How is Teal?" I ask, because it seems safer to deflect rather than talk about the very public turn my relationship with Cannon has taken.

Instead of giving me a look that could kill, Tanya's expression softens. "She's . . . she's getting the help she needs. Finally." Tanya glances at Cannon as he exchanges one of those handshakes that turns into a backslapping hug with a gray-haired man.

"I'm so sorry, Tanya. I had no idea what you were dealing with. I—"

"You just thought I hated you for getting hired. I know. Teal's not the only one who has amends to make. I've actually been meaning to talk to you because I did want to say I'm sorry for being such a bitch, but we've been so busy. Regardless, none of it was your fault. You just stepped into a shitty situation when my life was falling apart."

She shrugs and takes a sip of her drink.

"It was easy to blame you." Her hair falls into her face as her lips form a rueful smile. "I hope you'll forgive me. Maybe we can start over or something."

All of her body language tells me she's at least trying to be sincere.

"Thank you, Tanya. I appreciate that. And, of course I forgive you." I glance down at the bead of condensation streaking down the side of my glass. "My mother's an alcoholic. I get how hard it is to deal with addiction. It can be like a monster that just won't die. And when the person isn't willing to get help or even admit they have a problem . . ." I trail off. She knows that life as much as I do.

Tanya nods gravely. "Total clusterfuck. I'm really sorry you've had to deal with it too. I wouldn't wish it on anyone, especially someone who doesn't totally suck."

The corner of Tanya's mouth lifts, and I wonder if we've just bonded. Although I suspect we're light-years away from braiding each other's hair and swapping recipes, friendship between us isn't the worst thing that could happen.

"Same. Let me know if there's anything I can do to help with Teal. I really mean it."

She nods and lifts a glass to her lips to take another sip of what looks like ice water. "That means a lot. Have fun here. If you need to be rescued from some awkward conversation about how quickly you and Cannon are going to get married and start popping out perfect little bambinos, signal me and I'll try to help."

Before I can thank her for the surprising offer, she disappears into the crowd.

Cannon's arm slips around my hips, and I forget what I was going to say to her anyway. He pulls me into his side and lowers his head to whisper in my ear.

"Did I just hear Tanya apologize to you?"

"Are you as shocked as I am?"

He kisses my neck quickly enough that no one even sees him do it. "Not at all. She's good people. It was my fault that you got caught in her bitchy web over firing Teal. She would've hated anyone I hired. And then add in the fact that you're gorgeous and I pretty much couldn't stop myself from falling for you, it would give any woman in a shitty situation a reason to be pissed off. I shouldn't have put the target on your back for her."

"All of these apologies in one night. I'm not even sure what to do with them." I roll my shoulder into his chest and inhale his addictive scent.

"I would say put them in your pocket, but I suspect that dress you're wearing wasn't built to hold any more cargo than it's already got. You look fucking amazing tonight, baby. Just wait until I get you home."

I love when he flirts and plays. He's boyishly wicked, and I eat it up every time.

"I'm going to hold you to that."

"I dare you, but first brace yourself. Half the guest list isn't even here yet." As soon as he finishes speaking, his entire body stiffens and he straightens to his full height.

"What? What's wrong?" I follow his gaze to the entrance of the restaurant where a dark-haired man and a stunning brunette walk in the door. Every head in the room turns, as if on a swivel, to stare at them.

"Creighton and Holly are here."

Creighton Karas and Holly Wix. Cannon's former best friend and boss, who fired him once he found out that Cannon was really working for Dom and reporting back to him on all Creighton's actions. Oh, and current half brother, since they're both illegitimate sons of Dom—by different women.

I place my palm on his flat stomach and lean in. "Are you okay?"

Cannon's chin lifts as the other man's attention zeroes in on him. A silent conversation passes between them, one I can only imagine comes from half a lifetime of knowing each other well.

With what seems like Herculean effort, Cannon tears his attention away and looks down at me. "What?"

"Do you need me to run interference? So you don't have to deal with him?"

His face contemplative, Cannon seems to consider his response for longer than normal. "If Crey wants to talk to me, he will. Nothing and no one can stop that man from getting what he wants."

From the tone and respect in his voice, I would be willing to bet that Cannon wants to reconcile with Creighton, and badly. A lot of pent-up emotion is running through him, and for his sake, I wish we weren't in such a public place.

"Whatever you need me to do, I'll do it. All you have to do is tell me." It's the least I can do for the long nights he's stayed up with me, digging through my father's last investigation so we can bring it to a close.

Cannon leans down to brush a kiss across my lips. "Keep doing exactly what you're doing."

His answer is good enough for me, and I give him a smile that I hope fuels him through the night. "All right then. Do you want to mingle?"

"Cannon! It's been years, kid! How the hell are you?"

We both turn to face a man I now recognize from a picture in the file. *Benny Romano.* His tanned skin is lined with wrinkles, like he's spent his entire life outside without sunscreen.

"Benny, it's been too damn long. You're looking good." Cannon turns to hug the man and slap his back, which I'm thinking is pretty standard based on everything going on around me.

"When did you get older, kid? You're making me think *I'm* old, and I don't believe in that shit." He laughs, and it turns into a hacking and coughing fit. "Dammit. Excuse me."

"You're not old, Benny. You'll never be old."

"Damn right, because you're only as young as the women you feel." His gray eyes swing to me. "And speaking of which, who is this fox? I'd love to steal her right off your arm."

He holds out his hand, and instinctively, I take it.

"Sweetheart, you're a vision for sore, sore eyes. Why're you hanging out with this riffraff?"

I don't know if it's his navy-blue Hawaiian shirt or his gregarious personality, but I smile and laugh. "Maybe I like riffraff. I picked him out myself."

His eyes seem to twinkle. "Then you've come to the right place. Because we're all a little dangerous, baby."

Hearing the word *dangerous* has my eyes firing at Cannon's to briefly enjoy our inside joke. "Perfect, because I happen to love danger, Benny."

"Ha! I bet you do, doll." He wheezes through a chuckle. "I bet you do."

"Benny . . . tell me you're not rolling in from Florida to steal Cannon's girl. He fought hard for her, snagged her right out from beneath my nose."

Dom's low, rough voice pierces my levity, and I school my body not to stiffen. Benny releases my palm and turns to offer the mob boss his hand.

"Dominic. Seventy don't look half bad on you." Benny lifts the glass dangling from his free hand. "Cheers to making it beyond an early grave. It's good to see you, my friend."

"We'll let you two catch up," Cannon says, guiding me away from them. "We'll find you later, Benny. I'd love to hear more about where you got that shirt."

"Smartass kids these days. Should've beaten you more when I babysat," Benny jokes with a lift of his chin.

CHAPTER
NINETEEN

CANNON

I guide Memphis away from Benny and Dom as the restaurant fills to capacity. Andre's is your typical old-school Italian joint in the city, complete with red-and-white gingham tablecloths, brass fixtures, candles in little red glasses, and the scent of fresh basil and tomato sauce hanging in the air.

Dom's been coming here as long as I've been alive, as far as I know. He used to bring my mom here every Wednesday for lunch or dinner, and they'd sit in the back corner booth, where Dom did plenty of business—but never on Wednesdays. Wednesdays were always sacred for him.

I remember coming here with my mom as a kid too. But we always sat in the front, away from any mob business. It was her way of making sure Dom saw me, trying to get him to take an interest in me.

It worked too. When she passed, he inherited me like a bad debt. But I never lived with him. No, none of his illegitimate children were allowed into his home because of how his wife would react.

Yes, that's right. Dom had four secret bastard children, with four different women, while married to the same one the entire time. And his wife never once got pregnant before she died.

Karma's a bitch.

"Who's that woman staring at us?" Memphis asks, and I drag myself out of my trip down memory lane's back alley to follow her subtle stare across the room to the woman who isn't subtle about her staring at all.

Greer Karas. Or rather, Greer Westman. "That's Creighton's sister," I tell her, meeting Greer's gaze and giving her a subtle nod. "And no, she and I aren't related at all. Technically, she's Creighton's half sister. The *other* half."

Memphis tips her chin up at me, and her contacts slip to reveal a flash of aqua as she blinks. "Wait. What?"

I squeeze her hip and guide her toward the bar so she can replace her melted and only half-finished drink. "I should've given you a rundown on the twisted family tree before we came. Dom has four kids. We're all half siblings, even if we didn't all know it for most of our lives. Creighton and I are a few months apart. Cav is younger. He's Greer's husband, and you've definitely seen him before. He's a Hollywood hotshot now."

"Whoa. Whoa. Whoa. *Cav.* Like *Cavanaugh Westman?* How the hell didn't I know he was Dom's kid?" she whispers, and I'm thankful for the conversations and effusive greetings going on all around us, because Memphis's whisper might qualify as borderline yelling in her shock.

"Because there aren't any records you could dig up in your investigation. Not for any of us, except maybe Eden. She's the youngest by a lot. Dom was probably more a dad to her than anyone."

Quickly, Memphis slips that mask she's so damn good at using over her shocked face. "Okay, okay. I did find an Eden. And then Creighton. And you. But not a famous Hollywood actor." Her head swivels as I place an order with the bartender for both of us.

"He'll be near Greer, if you're looking to get a glimpse of the superstar."

Memphis's gaze swings right back to me, and it's with a healthy dose of side-eye. "I've interviewed plenty of celebrities. I'm not going to be starstruck. I just want to get a look at him in person to see if there's any resemblance between you two."

"Riiight," I reply with a roll of my eyes. "He's married. So, of course that's it."

Memphis reaches out to grip the knot of my tie. "Listen up, Danger. I'm only hot for you. Got it? Not some stuntman turned Hollywood heartthrob."

A throat clears behind us, followed by a giggle. "Good to know I don't have any competition for my husband."

Immediately, I lift my gaze to collide with Greer's. "It's been a while. You still hate me?" I ask, knowing her answer could go either way.

Back in the day, I was ordered to intervene in Greer's life when she and Cav were getting involved. It was an odd situation, considering I was taking Creighton's and Dom's orders at the same time, and Cav was ignoring everyone's. Not that Cav had answered to Dom in years.

I envied Cav and the freedom that his stardom afforded him. It just put him further out of Dom's reach and sliced most, and then all, of the strings tying him to our negligent father.

Growing up, Cav and I barely knew of each other's existence. He definitely didn't know I was Dom's bastard too. I can only assume Creighton has told Holly, Greer, and Cav by now.

Of course, I never let it out myself.

"Oh, shut up. I don't hate you, Cannon," Greer says, her gaze locked on mine. "We do miss you, though. Crey especially, even if he won't tell you himself. You two have to bury the hatchet, and preferably soon and not in each other's chest."

She knows us both well.

"It's good to see you, Greer. You look happy, despite being here."

Her smile slips a little, but her ability to hide her thoughts when in public has never been as well-honed as her brother's. "I didn't want to come. I didn't want Cav to come either. But he insisted that it was the right thing to do." She leans in, conspiratorially. "To be honest, I think he just wanted to rub that Academy Award in Dom's face."

A chuckle catches in my throat as she turns to Memphis.

Shit. I should have introduced them, but then again having a date—someone I care about by my side—is all new to me.

Before I can rectify my mistake, they're doing it for me.

"Hi, I'm Greer. It's really nice to meet any friend of

Cannon's." With her smiling introduction, she's fishing for information. Part of me wishes I could tell her the truth about Memphis, but that's not possible.

"Hello, it's nice to meet you—" Memphis begins, but I want there to be no mistaking what she is to me, so I interject.

"Greer, this is Drew, my girlfriend. Drew, this is Greer. I'd call her my little sister, except there's no blood shared between us."

"I think there's plenty of shared blood in this room without you and I being related. Besides, that would be gross." Greer shifts her gaze from me back to Memphis. "It's so nice to meet you. I'm shocked to see someone finally managed to tie down the uncatchable Cannon Freeman. I swore he'd never get serious with someone."

"Maybe he was just waiting for the *right* woman, like we all do." Cavanaugh Westman steps up behind his wife and wraps an arm around her middle before nodding at me in greeting. "Cannon. It's been a while." He holds out a hand and I shake it.

"It has. How are things? Congrats on the Academy Award." I can see the pride in his eyes, but he won't brag. It's not his style.

"Thanks. It was unexpected, which makes it that much better." And that's all he'll say about himself. Instead, he places a kiss to his wife's temple and asks me, "How are you doing? I heard from a friend you're managing the Upper Ten for dear old Dad."

Hearing someone say it out loud—in public—is something I may never get used to.

"Which friend is that?"

Cav's attention cuts from me to Memphis. "Silas Bohannon. We run in similar circles."

Greer whips around to look up at her husband. "Silas is here? Is Windsor?" Her gaze darts around the full room, scanning. "I seriously hope that those two get their heads out of their asses eventually and just hook up, for God's sake."

"Who's Windsor?" Memphis asks. This has to be a lot for her to take in, but she's yet to stumble or falter. She's unshakable.

Greer is more than happy to fill her in on the gossip. "Windsor Reed. She and Cav were costars in the *Casablanca* remake."

"Oh, wow. *That* Windsor." Memphis exhales the words with underlying shock. Windsor Reed is Hollywood royalty, and with Silas Bohannon being more of a Hollywood renegade, the two don't seem to mix at all.

"Windsor's good people. So is Bo," Cav says before squeezing his wife. "But Greer isn't going to meddle and try to bring them together. Are you, babe?"

Greer rolls her eyes, and I'm reminded of her rebellious streak. I wouldn't put it past her to push until she gets what she wants. The woman is scary smart and tenacious, and with a brother like Creighton Karas, she's a force to be reckoned with.

"Of course I won't interfere." In plain sight, she crosses her fingers and slips them behind her. "Unless I see an opening."

When Memphis laughs, I smile too.

"Wait until you see the gift that Crey and Cav got

together to give Dom. It's epic. He's going to lose his mind."

"What is it?" Memphis asks, but someone jostles me from behind, pushing through the crowd like a bull in a china shop.

Spinning to see who's being a dick, I'm not surprised in the least to see Enzo with a shitty expression on his face.

"Place is packed. Not that I'm surprised with so many Casso bastards jammed in here."

Cav stiffens as soon as he sees Enzo, and I wonder how many encounters he had with the douchebag while he was still living in the city. Hopefully, not many.

"You might want to lay off the drinks, Enzo. You're already looking a little red." My dig hits its mark, and his flushed face turns crimson. I don't know if it's the alcoholism or his blood pressure or just being a shitty human being, but he doesn't look healthy at all.

He attempts to look down his nose at me, but I'm taller and don't give a shit.

"I'm getting a drink for Dom. Mind getting out of the fucking way?"

His line is bullshit, because Andre's owner, Andre Canali, brings all Dom's drinks to him directly. Dom doesn't eat or drink anything from this place that isn't served by that man himself, and he hasn't in over twenty years. It started out as a gesture of trust, because Andre wanted Dom to feel comfortable here. By serving him the food personally, Andre acknowledged that if anything happened to Dom, his own life would be forfeit. Naturally, over the years they became friends, and the habit stuck.

Which means Enzo's trying to eavesdrop and doing a crap job at it, just like he does a crap job at everything else.

"Help yourself, Enzo." I grab our drinks off the bar and step back, leading Memphis away from the bustling area. Greer and Cav follow us.

"I've never liked that piece of shit," Cav says with a sharp glare aimed at the back of Enzo's head as the man unnecessarily elbows his way forward.

"He can't really be high up in the organization, can he? The man is just . . . *ewww*," Greer adds.

Cav looks down at her. "Probably not the best thing to talk about right here, if you know what I mean." He meets my eyes next, and it's proof that old habits die hard. Cav has spent enough time in the family to know that certain subjects never come up in public, and succession planning is one of them.

"So, what is this amazing gift you were talking about?" Memphis changes the subject like a pro, and Greer cranes her neck to look over the crowd toward the door.

"A car. A super-sweet, bomb-ass car. But they're not here yet. We told them to shoot for after dinner and cake. Given that Banner and Logan are pretty much almost late everywhere they go, I just hope they make it before the place clears out."

"What kind of car?" I ask, trying to shove down the hint of jealousy that rises inside me. Not only because I'm a collector, and if I had more room I could justify devoting to vehicles I don't drive often, I'd have a fleet instead of just a few that are my favorites. But also because Creighton and Cav went in on the gift together without asking me. They have to know I would have thrown some cash at it too.

"A 1964 Ferrari 275 GTB. Fully restored by a master. She's red and sleek and I've only seen pictures, but I'm still fucking jealous," Cav says.

I scan the room over Cav's shoulder to find Creighton and his wife, Holly, still besieged with partygoers-turned-fans to the point where they've barely made it beyond the entrance to the restaurant. He would insist that they give Dom something one of a kind. That's just Creighton's way. Another pang of regret slices into me at the loss of the friendship we'd had for years.

Through the whole duration of which, he never knew I was his brother. The impact of losing that connection seems even bigger now that I have time and perspective.

Dom's voice rises over the crowd as he calls out Creighton's name and makes his way over to him, telling everyone to back off and let his son in the door.

His son. The one he claims publicly, while Cav and I are afterthoughts.

I never cared before. My mother schooled me too well. *"Always do your best to make Dom happy. That's all that matters."*

But now I'm a full-grown man, and I'm fucking tired of trying to make someone happy who doesn't give a damn about me.

"That sounds incredible," Memphis says from beside me. "I guess it makes sense that he'd be into cars too."

But her words fall on deaf ears because Greer and Cav

are both staring in the same direction I am, watching Dom hug Creighton and clap him on the back like he's the long-lost son returned, when I know for a fucking fact that they had lunch two weeks ago.

"Well, this is awkward." Greer curls herself around her husband's side. "I'm sorry, babe. I don't know why he's like that with Crey and no one else."

"He's like that with Eden too, thankfully," Cav says. "Otherwise, Bishop would never let her come back to New York to see him."

I cut my gaze to my *other* half brother when he mentions our half sister. "Eden's really coming? I thought maybe they changed their minds at the last minute and decided to stay in New Orleans. I know Bishop isn't a fan of the city."

My half sister's husband is a giant of a guy with long hair he usually pulls back into a man bun, and he's covered with ink—some of which he did himself as he learned to be a tattoo artist. Now he's got one hell of a client list down in NOLA at a place called Voodoo Ink.

"She'll be here," Greer says. "We've kept in touch since Rose's baptism that Holly and Creighton had in Nashville."

A baptism I crashed, unwelcome, and begged for five minutes to speak with Creighton. It wasn't my proudest moment, but I'd gotten word of a competitor who was going to fuck him over.

Could I have sent an email? Sure.

Could I have sent a text or called? Absolutely.

Instead, I found myself flying to Tennessee anyway, busting into a family celebration that I should have been invited to—not as his second in command who he'd fired, but as the brother he didn't know he had.

Our conversation was short. He was pissed I dared interrupt a day for family, and rightly so. His next words filleted me like a fish.

"If you ever interrupt me at a family function again, even if it's to tell me you're dying, I'll have you railroaded out of the fucking country. You're already dead to me, Cannon. That's what happens to traitors."

I walked away without telling him I was sorry. It's the only thing I've wanted to tell him since, but my pride has kept me silent.

A delicate touch curls around my clenched fist at my side, and I loosen it so Memphis can thread her fingers through mine. I look down into her faux brown eyes, and although they're supportive, I wish I could see the aqua, but I smile. It starts out forced and then becomes genuine in a split second.

"Thank you," I tell her, not needing to explain why I'm so grateful. She gets it. Gets me.

And then Dom's voice drowns out everyone else's.

"My baby girl is back!"

CHAPTER TWENTY

I could skewer Dominic Casso where he stands. In front of all his friends and family. I wouldn't care at all that I'd be hauled off to jail immediately or, more likely, shot dead on the spot. Because with every excited outburst from the old man about his children, Cannon stiffens beside me like he's being stabbed.

What a motherfucking asshole of a father. Apparently, he missed the memo that you're supposed to treat your kids equally.

All four of us in our little group go silent as Cannon and his half brother Cav watch the father who apparently never gave much of a shit about them wrap a petite woman in a hug and lift her off the floor with the strength of a man half his age.

"Fucking dick," Greer whispers under her breath just loud enough for me to hear.

I make eye contact with her and nod in solidarity. I like her. I don't need to know another thing about her to know that she and I will get along fine.

Her brother is the golden boy in Dom's eyes, and her husband is an afterthought.

How fucking unfair?

But I doubt there's much use in trying to change a mobster's ways when he's just joined the septuagenarian club. That doesn't mean I wouldn't still try, and I have a feeling she would do the same.

"Anyone else hoping the car delivery gets delayed, and he doesn't get a shiny new toy tonight?" The words are out of my mouth before I remind myself to shut the hell up.

Thankfully, Cannon squeezes my hand before looping his arm around me. He and Cavanaugh Westman both laugh, and Greer giggles.

"That can definitely be arranged. I know all of Banner's dirty secrets, and I'm not above blackmail." Greer winks at me, and I reaffirm my opinion—I definitely like her.

Cannon says again, "It's so damn good to see you, Greer. New York has missed you."

She reaches out to shove Cannon's shoulder in a very sibling-like gesture. "You mean you've missed me and you're just too proud to say it."

"Not too proud at all. I've missed you like hell. Nothing's been the same since . . ." Cannon trails off because the elephant in the room stops right beside us.

"Greer. Cav. I was hoping you were already here. Come see Holly. She's missed you and was worried you wouldn't make it."

Creighton Karas, notorious billionaire and Cannon's ex-best friend yet still half brother, stands a few feet away, and a rush of emotion swirls through me like a twister. It's like Cannon and I are totally invisible to him.

I've never been so torn on what to do in my entire life.

Greer asks her brother, "Crey, have you met Drew? She's Cannon's girlfriend."

His dark eyes land on me, skipping over Cannon completely. His face is blank, showing no emotion at all.

"You should be careful with the company you keep." And then he turns and walks away.

Oh. My. Fucking. God.

Beside me, Cannon jerks his hand from mine and takes two steps after Creighton before being waylaid by someone as Creighton cuts through the crowd.

"What a fucking dick," Greer says.

"Babe—" Cav's voice is full of concern and warning.

Greer shakes her head. "No. That was uncalled for. They have to talk and have it out. I'm tired of this shit. Cannon didn't have a choice in what he did, and if Crey thinks that he would be where he is today *without* Cannon working his ass off beside him all those years, he's insane."

I search for Cannon again in the crowd, partly hoping he caught up with Creighton and they're going to have it out right now, but I'm not so lucky.

He's gone.

Greer and her husband politely invite me to stick with them as they circulate through the party, but since I assume they're going to talk to Holly and Creighton, I respectfully decline. They leave me with a promise to find me later, and Greer insists we need to get together for dinner and drinks before they leave town. I tell her I'd love that, and we exchange phone numbers before I make my way back to the bar.

I don't plan on drinking much tonight, but it's either fill my time with another drink or hang out in the corner, pretending I don't feel awkward at being abandoned.

And it's not the desertion part that bothers me. Not at all. If Cannon hadn't gone after Creighton, I would have shoved him in his direction anyway. Those two clearly need some time to talk and bury the hatchet. I just hope they don't do it literally, like Greer said.

At the bar, Benny from Boca sidles up beside me in his loud Hawaiian shirt. "Hey, pretty girl. How about I buy you a drink?"

He laughs at his last statement because it's an open bar, but I politely grin and nod anyway. I could use some company to kill a little time.

"I would appreciate that, sir."

He shakes his head, and the bit of gray still hanging on around the edges flaps with the movement. "I'm no sir. Just Benny. Anything else makes me feel old, and I refuse to believe that horseshit."

The man is seventy-five if he's a day, and probably even a bit older, but I'm not about to ask him.

"I like your attitude, Benny. What's it like being back in New York after being gone for a while?"

He tilts his head from side to side while signaling the besieged bartenders. Knowing it's going to be a while, I settle in for the conversation to come by scooting my skirt-clad butt onto a stool, and Benny does the same.

"Things have changed a lot. Buildings I remember being here are gone, and there's skeletons of something new in their place. I miss the old days, when people weren't walking while staring at their phones. They stared at the sidewalk like proper New Yorkers, avoiding eye contact on purpose, but at least they didn't run into you because they're oblivious."

I can't help but laugh because it's the truth. I almost saw a woman get nailed by a cab as she stepped into a crosswalk when the light turned, all because she was too busy looking at her phone to notice.

"Maybe it's a new version of survival of the fittest, except this time, only the aware survive and the oblivious remove themselves from the gene pool."

Benny's laugh sounds like a crumpling paper grocery sack, which immediately morphs into him coughing up a lung. I nab a *Dom turns 40 for the 30th time* water bottle from the arrangement on the bar, unscrew the cap, and slide it in front of him.

"Thanks, gorgeous." The old guy wipes his mouth with a handkerchief he pulled from his pocket, and I don't miss the smear of blood on it before he folds it and tucks it away.

Fucking hell. That's not good.

He sips from the bottle and makes a disgusted face.

"Something wrong with the water?" I ask, wondering if I handed him one that was tainted or something.

"No whiskey in it. That's what's wrong."

This time I smile and push out a chuckle. "You sound like a man set in his ways."

"We all are. But sometimes, if the right woman comes

along, we make room for change." He shoots me a thoughtful look, and at that moment, I realize he sought me out on purpose.

"You sound like you've got something on your mind, Benny. Lay it on me."

His teeth may be false, but the grin is genuine. "You're direct. I like that in a woman. I see how Cannon got wrapped up in you."

"Are you going to warn me away from him too? Because it's a little too late for that."

In an instant, Benny's entire face changes into a cold, hard mask, and it's like I'm staring at a different person.

"Not if you've got ill intentions toward my boy, it's never too late. He's been through a special kind of hell. Never had an identity of his own. Always following orders. No freedom on the horizon until now, and I'm not about to let him get sucked in by some woman who isn't going to treat him like the prince he is. I'll put her in the ground first."

Chills ripple over every single inch of my body. The hair on the back of my neck stands on end. Cold sweat breaks out across my chest.

Benny wasn't a good-time guy.

Benny was a killer.

I don't know how I know that, but I feel it straight to the marrow of my bones.

Even though he vaguely said, "I'll put her in the ground first," he's talking about me. This old man, who is coughing up blood and probably knows about how many days he's got left on this planet, is threatening to murder me, and he's serious.

Hell, if he knew how Cannon and I got started, he'd probably kill me right here, in front of an entire restaurant full of witnesses who would no doubt testify that they'd seen nothing, had never met me, and give each other alibis. *Isn't the mob great?*

I have two choices right now. I can either run, or I can face him and try to make him my ally. *God knows I could use one.*

Sitting up straighter on the stool, I meet his faded gaze. "I'd put her in the ground before you could, Benny."

The mask of the killer disappears from his face like it was never there. Once again, a jovial old man sits on the stool beside me, and his lips curl up with a cocky smirk.

"That's what I thought. I like you, Drew. And trust me, I'd hate to have to clip a pretty flower like yourself, so young and full of life, but I will if I have to."

Those chills I felt before? They're back with a vengeance. Something about him making that promise to me with a smile on his face is even more disturbing than the blank mask of a killer.

"I'd really hate that too. Especially since I'm in love with Cannon, and I only want the best for him."

The bartender finally stops in front of us, and Benny orders a whiskey neat and gestures to me.

"I'll have the same."

One corner of Benny's mouth quirks up as the bartender disappears again.

"What?" I ask him with a smile.

"There's just something about you. Especially the way your eyes turn turquoise when you blink."

Fucking hell. He knows I'm wearing colored contacts.

Apparently taking refuge at the bar was a terrible decision. Actually, me coming to this party was terrible decision number one.

"Why are you hiding yourself, kid? Cannon know about this?"

I nod. "Yes. He knows everything."

"Good, because—"

"Because you'd hate to have to kill me."

"Got it in one." He narrows his gaze at me and makes a strange request. "Can you move that contact for a second? I want to see the real color of your eyes."

I don't know why I humor him, but I put my middle finger on the contact and slide it sideways for a second and then let it go back into place, blinking a few times until it's sitting comfortably again.

"Fucking hell. I ain't seen eyes that color in over twenty-five years. And only on one woman ever."

My heartbeat pounds in my ears, and my limbs feel heavy, like my body knows something is coming, even though I have no clue what he's going to say. "On what woman?"

The bartender returns and slides our drinks across the bar to us.

Benny wraps his tanned and age-spotted paw around his whiskey glass before meeting my gaze once more. "A dead one."

CHAPTER TWENTY-ONE

"When are you going to throw your hat in the ring and give Enzo some real competition for when Dom steps down?"

It's the fucking question of the night, apparently. First from Junior Gallo as he jumped in my way when I was going after Creighton, and then from Paulie Salerno, who found me in the bathroom while I was taking a piss.

All I want to do is get back to Memphis, make sure she's doing okay, and then force Creighton to finally have the come-to-Jesus talk that we've been due to have for a long fucking time.

But of course, it doesn't matter what I want.

I'm sick and tired of this shit. Maybe I should take over the family, for the sole purpose of getting everyone to finally give a damn about what *I* want.

Since I came back into the fold to manage the Upper Ten, I've been in this limbo stage where I'm not *in* but I'm also not *out,* because I'm in charge of the biggest legit Casso cash cow.

Still, no one knows how to treat me, and they revert to treating me like the bastard kid Dom won't acknowledge publicly, which makes me fair game for prying questions. I'm done with it.

"I'm my own man, Paulie. I'll do whatever the fuck I want when the time comes."

Paulie jerks a paper towel out of the dispenser and leers at me. "You ain't your own man. You never have been. You've always answered to the king and you always will—unless you take control." There's no way he's saying any of this without a motive.

I march to the wooden stalls and slap open both doors to make sure there's no one else in the bathroom to overhear our conversation, but even seeing that we're in the clear, I won't say much. There's a chance Andre has the bathrooms bugged. A damn good chance, actually.

I cross my arms over my chest and face Paulie head-on. "What's your angle? You and Junior talk about this shit before you got here? Both of you are hard up for an answer. Why aren't either of you trying to take control if you want Enzo out so bad?"

As Paulie's jaw shifts from side to side, I'm reminded that he's been a capo for a couple of years, but for some reason, Dom favors Enzo over him. Paulie's also not used to having someone talk to him like this, unless that someone is Dom.

"Dom wants his blood to take over."

I stare at him, blinking rapidly as I try to put the pieces together.

No fucking way.

"You're telling me Enzo is Dom's bastard too?"

Paulie's paranoia has his eyes darting to the door, as if he's afraid what I just said will summon the devil himself.

"Not Dom's. I think we all agree he spread his seed far enough as it is."

My patience is running thin. "Then what the fuck are you saying about blood? Enzo isn't fucking related."

Paulie moves closer and fidgets with another wipe of his thumb across his nose. "Enzo says he is. Says he's got a DNA test proving he's Dom's nephew."

What in the actual fuck? "When did he get the test, and how the hell did I not know this?"

"Why the fuck do you think Enzo got made?" Paulie says, his words underlined by his personal frustration. "And if I recall, you weren't exactly in the loop with Dom's decisions back then. Or now."

"You've gotta be fucking kidding me. *That's* why that fucking idiot is Dom's number two? Because of a DNA test that Enzo's probably smart enough to pay off someone to fake?" I shake my head and consider what he's telling me. "Dom had one sister. She was a *fucking nun until she died.* How the hell did Enzo get Dom to buy that she had a kid?"

Paulie's dark eyebrows, threaded with hints of silver, rise to his hairline. "Apparently, she joined the convent because she got in the family way, and no one knew about it because she gave up the baby for adoption. Enzo claims he's that baby."

"*Fucking hell.* This changes everything."

Paulie nods slowly. "Sure as fuck does, which is why we need to know that you're our man. Because there's no chance in hell Cav and Creighton will walk away from their lives to run the organization. No one would follow a woman, so Eden's out. That leaves you and Enzo. And I think we all know who we'd rather have at the top of the food chain." Paulie sucks in a big breath and releases it just as slowly. "Enzo would get us all killed. Even you see that."

It's the truth. I have zero doubt in my mind that Enzo would be the death of us and possibly the entire Casso name, especially since Dom declared that we're going to war with the Rossettis. Enzo is practically foaming at the mouth to snuff out GTR's dad just to prove a point.

And that's exactly when all hell would break loose.

"Fucking hell," I say again, turning to lean on the sink. I stare at my reflection. It's the same face I see every fucking day, but now there's another question I have to answer.

Am I looking at a mobster . . . or at a businessman who needs to cut ties with the family completely while I still can?

Paulie walks over and claps me on the shoulder. "Think about it, Cannon. We'll support you. Respect you. Follow you. You could take us to a new level. Kick some of the petty shit. I don't know that I could go legit, but if you wanted to take us in that direction, I'd give it a shot and wouldn't argue." His gaze meets mine in the mirror.

"Thanks for that, man."

"You've got a lot to think about. Just know that it's not only your life on the line here. I'd like to live long enough to retire in Boca like Benny. You're my only hope of that happening."

He backs away and returns to the party, leaving me

leaning on the counter, collecting my fucked-up thoughts during a rare minute of blessed silence.

At least, the bathroom is largely silent. My mind is the site of a riot.

What the fuck am I going to do?

The door to the bathroom swings open and in walks the last person I want to see right now. *Enzo.*

I push off the black-and-white-specked countertop and stride to the paper towel dispenser as he turns to the urinal to take a piss.

Deciding I don't have a fucking thing to say to him, I head for the door. As soon as my hand touches the knob, Enzo breaks the silence.

"I don't give a fuck what Paulie and Junior want. This family is mine. I'll kill you before I'll let you take it from me."

"Go fuck yourself, Enzo." I yank the door open and let it slam shut behind me as I stride out—right into Dom.

"Something wrong?" my father asks, and I move out of his way.

"Not a damn thing."

His dark eyes sharpen on me, and I know he doesn't believe a word I'm saying.

"I'm hearing talk tonight. Lots of talk."

I shrug and straighten my jacket. "About what?" Playing the fool is a role he expects from me.

"Conversations that shouldn't be happening on my goddamned birthday. But Monday, you and I are gonna sit down. Talk about the future. I didn't spend my whole life building something to let other people make my fucking decisions now. Understand me?"

I know he's waiting for a *yes, sir, I understand* response, but I'm not giving him that. Not tonight. I don't care that it's his fucking birthday.

"Monday it is, then. Excuse me, I need to find my woman."

Dom's expression takes on a chilling glare. "Yeah, Drew with the laugh. You better know what the fuck you're doing with her because she's a fine piece, and I'd hate for something bad to happen to her."

Everything drops away but the man in front of me. The room goes silent. Every party attendee disappears. It's just me and Dom and his vague threat against Memphis hanging in the room. A threat I won't stand for.

I meet his gaze with no deference in my expression whatsoever. Regardless of what Paulie said, I am my own man when it matters. And I won't let anyone touch Memphis.

I pitch my voice low but make sure every fucking word comes out clear. "If anything happens to her on your orders, I'll retire you myself."

Something sparks in Dom's gaze, and there's a chance it's murderous rage. Or it could be respect. Right now, I don't fucking care about anything but letting him know that Memphis is off-limits.

"She's hooked you good." His hand lands on my shoulder, much the same way Paulie's did, but Dom squeezes hard to get his point across. "Don't ever fucking talk to me like that again or you'll pay the price, *son.*"

CHAPTER TWENTY-TWO

"**A** *dead one.*"

My eyes, the color of which I've never seen on another person, are a perfect match for those a retired mob hit man remembers on a woman who died twenty-five years ago.

The revelation sends me reeling.

For my entire life, I've wondered how my brown-eyed father could have had a daughter without brown eyes, but I always chalked it up to my mysterious biological mother. The one I've never searched for due to my father's wishes, despite my intense curiosity. But what if . . .

No. That's impossible. Still, the reporter in me needs more information.

"What . . . what was her name?"

Benny sips his whiskey while he studies my face, looking for answers of his own. "Why do you want to know?"

I shift casually on my seat, not wanting to give too

much away, and lift my glass to my lips. "Wouldn't you want to know if a tall, dark, and handsome man told you'd he'd only seen eyes like yours on one woman?" Flattery might not get me everywhere, but hopefully it will afford me more than I have now, which is only unanswered questions.

"Fair enough, but only because a beautiful woman is asking. Her name was Regina, and she was a knockout. Long black hair, piercing turquoise eyes. If you dyed your hair dark and ditched those contacts, you could be sisters. Granted, she didn't live much longer than however old you are now. Real sad story."

If I dyed my hair dark . . .

Blood roars in my ears at his statement. I should be happy that he hasn't caught on to the fact that I'm wearing a wig, but my fingers itch to rip it off so he can see the real me. The me who has never known my biological mother.

But my father has always kept an apartment in New York.

This is too little to go on, but it's more than I've ever had before. A million questions rush through my brain, but I only ask one.

"How did she die?"

Benny coughs and wipes his mouth again with his handkerchief. He doesn't answer until he's refolded it and tucked it away. "She was murdered."

My heart hammers harder than ever before, each beat slamming into my chest like a bare-knuckle punch. I open my mouth to reply but Greer's cheerful voice stops me, and I don't know if I'm grateful or pissed.

"Drew! I wondered where you'd disappeared to. There's someone I would love to introduce you to."

I break Benny's stare and glance at Greer, but her face doesn't match her voice. Her expression is lined with concern, and I wonder if she's trying to rescue me. *Do I want to be rescued?*

Her bright gaze bounces from me to Benny. "Oh, I'm sorry. I didn't mean to interrupt."

"It's all right, sweetheart. We're just talking about ancient history. I'm sure she'd rather meet your talented sister-in-law. I'm just gonna say, if Ms. Superstar doesn't sing 'Happy Birthday' to Dom, we're all gonna be mighty disappointed." He sips at his liquor like it truly does go down easier than water.

I turn to see Holly Wix, one of country music's hottest stars, standing beside Greer.

How the hell didn't I notice her before? Oh, right, I was having a meltdown and wondering if Benny knows who my biological mother is, and *oh, just maybe she might have been some woman who was murdered.*

Using compartmentalization skills I've honed since childhood, I tuck my questions away in a box, pop off the bar stool, and hold out my hand to the gorgeous brunette who came into the restaurant with Creighton Karas.

"It's a pleasure. I'm a huge fan of your music. I saw you perform once at a concert in LA. You were incredible." I'm thankful my words come out sounding coherent rather than discombobulated, like I feel.

Instead of taking my hand, Holly reaches out with both arms and wraps them around me. "Oh my goodness, I'm so damn grateful that Cannon has finally found someone who can handle his cranky ass. Welcome to the family. We've been waiting for you a long, long time."

Her citrus-and-sunshine scent wraps around me, chasing the chills away. Over her shoulder, Benny gives me a chin jerk, slides off his stool with his drink, and disappears into the crowd.

I'm not sure if I just received a stay of execution or lost a chance at learning something vital, but I don't have time to think about it right now.

"Thank you," I say, scrambling for words.

Greer smiles and laughs, clearly happy to see Holly embracing me.

"Oh, girl, don't thank me," Holly says as her arms unwind from around me and she steps back. "I was just so glad to hear when Greer told me about you. I've been waiting years for this moment. You don't even know."

"Maybe now they can finally make up and have their bromance back," Greer adds with hope in her voice. "I know Creighton has been missing Cannon like a lost limb, even though he denies it."

"Of course he has. Do you know how many times Crey picks up his phone to call and tell Cannon something and then sets it down when he realizes he deleted his number? It's worse than a teenage girl with a breakup." Holly shakes her head, and her dark waves dance around her shoulders.

She's even more beautiful in person than on TV, and that's definitely a surprise. I've met so many famous people in my life, and they always look different without the heavy layers of makeup that get them camera ready.

"Speaking of Crey, where is he?" Greer asks, turning to scan the restaurant.

At the same time, silverware clinks on a glass somewhere. As the hum of conversation subsides, all heads swivel to find the source.

It's Dom. He stands at one of four tables that have been set for dinner, each about ten feet long, with enough room to accommodate the fifty or so people who have been milling around and making small talk.

When the room goes silent and he has everyone's attention, a smile stretches over his face like he's a king surveying his subjects, which I suppose is how he feels. Here, he's a god. No one outranks him. His decision is the final word on all things. One must wonder if having that kind of power for years would go to someone's head, and from the way Dom takes no shit, I would have to think it absolutely has.

"Family and friends, thank you all for coming this evening. I think many of you doubted I'd ever live to see this birthday, but I'm happy to prove you wrong."

As everyone chuckles at Dom's statement, my gaze skips over the crowd, trying to find Cannon, and I spot him near the exit. He's a dozen feet from Creighton, but the other man has his back to Cannon.

I wish I could fix things for them. After hearing Greer and Holly, I'm more convinced than ever that it's crucial the breach in their friendship be mended.

"Now please sit, eat, and drink because we are on the edge of a new era. The next time we gather, I'll share my plans for the future. But tonight—tonight we *celebrate*!"

Dom lifts his glass in the air, and the crowd cheers and does the same.

Someone calls out "Salud," and everyone shouts it before taking a sip and maneuvering around one another to take their seats.

Greer's husband, Cav, arrives beside us and leans his head low, but he speaks loud enough for me to overhear. "Dom wants us to sit at his table. You, me, Eden, Bishop, Holly, and Creighton."

"But what about—" Greer shoots a look at me, and I know what she's thinking. *Cannon*, the outcast son once again.

My heart pinches at the thought of him not getting to sit with the others. It's not like he's the only illegitimate child. They're *all* illegitimate.

Screw the pain in my chest. A fire borne of rage ignites in my belly, and I want to march right up to Dom and tell him that he's being an asshole by treating Cannon the way he does. If he can't respect Cannon and treat him as an equal with all his other children, then Dom doesn't deserve to have Cannon managing something as important as the Upper Ten.

I have money. Cannon has money. We could open our own club. Screw Dom and his reign. I won't spend the rest of my life watching Cannon being ignored like he doesn't matter, when he should be the most important person in this goddamned room to everyone.

Whoa. I went there.

The rest of my life. That's how long I want Cannon with me.

The realization should be scary. Frightening. Terrifying.

But it's not. It just feels *right.*

Given my thoughts, it only makes sense that the man himself would be standing beside me before I have more than a moment to collect myself. I stare up at his face, noting every variance of his hazel eyes, which are greener tonight than normal.

"We can go if you want," I tell him.

Cannon's expression creases with confusion as he slides his arm around me and rests his palm on the small of my back. "Do you want to go?"

"If Dom isn't going to put you at the same table with all your half siblings, then yeah, I do. Because that's bull-shit." My indignation comes through loud and clear in my tone. "I won't let him treat you like that. Not today. Not ever again."

His expression softens with a smile, and it transforms his entire face. "You look like a fury, ready to go to battle for me over this."

I swallow the lump in my throat. "I would go to battle for you over just about anything. You're my person, Cannon. I'm not going to stand by and let him—"

"Cannon."

Dom's voice breaks into my tirade, and I go silent, hoping like hell his next words aren't going to make me want to kill him.

"Come sit with the family."

Relief sweeps over me. *Thank God.*

"You sure?" Cannon stiffens beside me. I can only

imagine how much he wants this. How important this is to him.

Dom waves at the last two open seats near him. "It's where you belong. Come on. The food will be out in a minute."

That's how I found myself being seated across the long table from Holly Wix with Cannon at my side.

The doors from the kitchen fling open and the wait-staff march out in a line, carrying heavy trays loaded with salads.

I scan down either side of the table, but there's no sign of Creighton. Holly shifts in her seat, searching for her husband too. As soon as a salad is placed in front of me, the tall, dark-haired man appears next to his wife, his hand on the back of the chair across from Cannon.

My entire body goes still as the two men face each other.

"Crey, sit. Eat." Holly's voice carries just a hint of her Southern accent, making it lyrical and sweet, but her husband stands unmoving like a block of marble as he stares at his former best friend.

His knuckles turn white, and everyone in the room seems to hold their breath.

CHAPTER TWENTY-THREE

When you're ordered to befriend someone when you're barely a teenager, it's not a job. It's your life.

I've known Creighton Karas for over twenty years, and never once did I tell him that we were brothers.

Never. Once.

But with him staring me down, dozens of emotions flying across his features, chief among them anger and betrayal, I've had enough of the rift between us. I don't care that everyone is watching like we're the main event on a fight card. I say what I need to say, because I'm tired of holding back the words.

"I'm not sorry, Crey. I'd do it all again. I wouldn't trade that twenty-odd years for anything. You can hate me for the rest of your life, if you want, but I'd do it all again."

In an instant, Creighton's face morphs into a polite mask, devoid of emotion, as he pulls out his chair, unbuttons his suit jacket, and sits. "I don't know what you're talking about," he says and then turns to say something to Holly, shutting me out.

Beside me, Memphis slides her hand onto my knee and squeezes in support, and I want to flip this table and force him to talk to me. But I know better than anyone how cold and hard Creighton Karas can be. He had no choice but to grow up with his emotions locked in a dungeon, just like I did.

We might not have been raised the same—me on Dom's afterthoughts of generosity, and him in the lap of luxury with his wealthy relatives—but we both experienced emotional terrorism that forged us into the men we are today.

From the other end of the table, Eden waves at me with a smile. *At least two-thirds of my siblings are happy I exist.* I tell myself that's enough for me, but I know I'm full of shit.

Because right now, I need Creighton more than I've ever needed him before. Who the hell else can I talk to about this fucking mess with Enzo and Dom wanting one of us to take over the family? No one knows me better than Creighton. No one understands the position I'm in quite like he does.

And yet, the one person whose advice I want more than anything is completely closed off to me because I followed orders.

I'm done following fucking orders.

With all these comments tonight about me not being my own man unless I take over, I find my decision is getting harder, not easier.

Can I walk away and leave everything to Enzo? If the

capos don't support him, how can he possibly lead?

I would love to think that he couldn't and one of them would rise up to replace him, but I know that's not the case. Enzo wouldn't risk losing power as quickly as he gained it. No, he'd make a show of dominance. A bloody one. Like executing all his opposition and daring anyone else to question his right to lead.

And in this world, that's what men follow.

Dom's gaze is on me as I eat my salad, and I know he wants in my head. What would he say if I told him *I don't fucking want this?*

He would turn his back on me in an instant. *Wouldn't he?* And why the fuck do I care? I'm a grown-ass man, and I don't need my father's approval.

But still, a voice inside me asks another question. *But wouldn't it feel fucking good to finally command their respect?*

For years, I've been at the bottom of the food chain. No one knows what to make of me. For once, it would be really fucking nice to have everyone know exactly where I stand and where their loyalty belongs.

I find Memphis's hand beneath the table and tangle our fingers together.

But could I do that to her? She's not meant to be the wife of a mobster.

Wife.

The word echoes in my mind through the meal. No one notices that I stay quiet rather than fill the air with chatter like the rest of the table, except for the eyes I feel boring into the back of my head.

That's when it hits me. *I'm not the one being pushed aside tonight.* With a glance over my right shoulder, I confirm that Enzo stares daggers my way from the table with the capos who don't want him to lead.

Enzo says he's family, but Dom put all the family at one table. Is this Dom's way of making a statement?

I meet my father's gaze, but he's too busy laughing and trading stories with Eden and Greer at the other end of the table for me to get a read on him.

I count the chairs. Five on one side. Four on the other.

If he'd wanted Enzo at this table, with the *family*, there was room for another chair.

It is a statement. I'd stake my life on it. *Now, what the hell am I going to do about it?*

We're finishing up the main course when Greer pulls out her phone and smiles. She gives Creighton a nod, and he stands.

"Dom, if you'd like, your birthday present from all of us is here and ready for you to see."

The old man's face lights up like a kid on Christmas morning, and I try to shove down the jealousy that *all of us* doesn't include me.

"Of course I want to see it. I can eat Andre's veal parm any damn time." He looks from side to side. "Where's it at? They bringing it inside?"

Crey points at the door. "It's outside. You definitely don't want it coming in."

Dom pops out of his seat with the agility of a man half his age. "Then we're going outside." He holds out his arms to signal to the rest of the attendees. "Come on, it's time for my gift. Let's go see what it is."

The entire crowd funnels toward the doors, and

Memphis and I are a few people back from Dom when we hear a woman yell, "Happy birthday, Dom!"

When we reach the sidewalk, a flatbed fifth-wheel trailer hooked up to a massive black dually truck is parked at the curb. On the flatbed is a car, sheltered under a cover with a giant red bow on top. Banner and Logan Brantley stand in front of the trailer with huge smiles on their faces.

Banner, no doubt, because she gets to see Greer—who rushes off the sidewalk to wrap her best friend in a hug. And Logan must be grinning because he made *bank* on this project. His restorations aren't cheap. I would know, because he's working on one for me right now. It doesn't matter that he's all the way down in Kentucky. He's the best.

Dom stands on the edge of the walkway, staring at the car. He turns around and glances at Creighton, his eyes wide, and more excited than I've ever seen him. I shove down the anger at being excluded from the gift and embrace the moment.

Dom's happy, and that's not something we see often.

"Well, let's see it!" Dom shouts at the head of the small crowd.

Creighton nods at Logan, who steps up onto the trailer and holds out his hand for Banner. Together they work to remove the cover slowly, so we can all savor the unveiling. As soon as the shiny red paint catches the light and the Ferrari logo is unveiled, Dom's mouth drops open.

The old man claps his hands more like a seven-year-old than a seventy-year-old when he realizes what he's looking at. "That's a 275 GTB. *Holy shit.*"

As Dom walks forward to run a hand along the perfectly waxed and buffed rear quarter panel, I catch a glimpse of a black Charger parked across the street, its windows tinted so dark you can't see in them.

I'd be willing to bet that sitting inside that car, behind those tinted windows, is Clinton Cole or one of his buddies, surveilling the entire fucking party.

Welcome to the mob, where your every family, birthday, and holiday gathering is watched and photographed by the cops.

"She's a 1964," Logan says. "Creighton and Cav said you'd always wanted one, so we found it for you and did a little work to make her shine."

Knowing Logan, he's vastly understating the amount of effort it took to get the car to this condition, but Dom is too busy skimming his fingertips across the paint to care.

"Best fucking birthday I've ever had. Nothing after this will ever—"

Dom's head jerks to the side, cutting off his words, as gunfire erupts.

CHAPTER TWENTY-FOUR

"Down!" Dom yells the word, and the entire crowd of people freezes for a second before following his instructions.

As the *rat-tat-tat* of automatic weapon fire fills the air and glass shatters everywhere, I throw myself at Cannon, sending us both tumbling to the ground. He tries to shield me as he moves us toward the tires of the truck, and I reach out my hand to Dom, trying to catch him and drag him closer to cover. Cannon sees what I'm trying to do and shoves me lower as he grabs his father's arm and pulls him toward us.

Dom's face is bleached white and he already has a gun in his hand, but he's frozen beside us as we huddle behind the tire.

Gunfire breaks out from our side of the street, and I don't want to move my head to see who's shooting at who. With every explosion deafening me, I cringe into a smaller and smaller ball, thankful for the thud of Cannon's beating heart against me.

I can't lose him. I won't lose him. No matter what.

Tires squeal, and the acrid scent of gunpowder mingles with the stench of burning rubber.

For a moment, all I hear is the ringing in my ears along with the whoosh of blood.

Cannon's grip on me tightens when I try to move. "No, stay down. They could come back. Sometimes they fucking come back."

But instead of more squealing tires, sirens wail in the distance as people begin shouting.

"Gotta. Follow. Them."

The stilted, wheezy words come from Dom, and I shift to see the older man's face. I've never seen a living person's face turn that color gray. One of his hands clutches the lapel of his jacket . . .

Oh Jesus Christ. No.

"Cannon! Cannon! We need an ambulance. Now!"

He replies, his voice cloaked in dread, "We're going to need more than one."

"Dom needs one. Right now. *Right now!*"

Other people are yelling for help, but Cannon's attention is on his father.

"My heart," Dom says before letting his eyes flutter shut.

I stand up, screaming for help, but my shouts disappear in the chaos. It's a war zone. Blood stains clothes and the sidewalk.

"I got every bus I can find coming this way."

I look toward the voice, stunned to see Clinton Cole standing beside me.

"Help's coming," he says.

"Who . . ." Dom opens his eyes, and Cannon cradles him in his lap. "Did you see who . . ."

Benny drops to his knees beside Cannon. "It was that fucking bastard GTR. We're gonna kill the Rossettis. Every single damn one of them. Put them in the fucking ground."

"Damn . . . right . . . we are." Dom meets Cannon's gaze, and I'm terrified he won't be able to hold on long enough for the ambulance to arrive.

"I'm gonna kill 'em all." Enzo stumbles to a stop near Benny, his shirt stained with blood, one hand pressed to his side and the other holding a gun. "Then you'll know I'm worthy."

"Save your declarations of war for when you don't have a cop standing right in front of you, assholes," Cole says as Enzo tilts to one side and clutches at Cole to stay up.

Eden rushes toward us and throws herself into Cannon's arms. "Greer and Crey both got hit. We need help. Now!"

CHAPTER TWENTY-FIVE

CANNON

I hate hospitals. Everything about them. From the white walls, to the industrial floors, to the scent of disinfectant. Most of all, I hate that you walk inside with a sense of hope, only to get robbed of it later when the doctor comes out to give you the bad news.

It isn't the same hospital I sat in, waiting for news about my mother in surgery, but it might as well be.

Dom didn't get capped, but his heart couldn't handle the stress. Creighton, Enzo, and four others were shot. Greer caught some flying glass, but thankfully not a bullet. How the rest of us survived unscathed while the Rossettis were shooting at us like fish in a barrel, I'll never understand.

Grace of God, I guess.

The entire waiting room is packed with people I've known my entire life, or most of it, waiting on the same news.

Will the king survive?

Memphis gets up to go to the restroom with Holly,

who's barely holding it together, and Benny sits down beside me.

"You know he's been having heart problems, right?" he asks.

"What?" I whip my head to the side. "No. He never said anything."

With a nod, Benny dangles his paper coffee cup from one hand. "He's been seeing a doctor regularly for it over the last year. Been too stubborn to take the doc's advice. Couldn't wrap his head around the downtime. Didn't want to show weakness at such a sensitive time."

"And he told you all this? Shit, I can't believe he told anyone." *Show no weakness* might as well be the creed that Dominic Casso lives by. And possibly dies by, coincidentally.

"He only told me because, well, he knows I'm not gonna be here long enough to tell anyone else. But you deserve to know too, kid," Benny says.

"What do you mean?"

His gaze dips to the floor before coming up to meet mine. "You don't live like I did and get to have a happily-ever-after. Karma's a bitch, and she always takes her due. I've got lung cancer. Terminal. Maybe six or eight months, if I'm lucky."

"Jesus, Benny. Why didn't you say anything?"

He shrugs, his shoulders appearing bonier than ever under the blue Hawaiian shirt, now that I'm really looking. "Not shit anyone can do. I'm not fighting it. I deserve it. Hell, I deserve worse for all the terrible things I've done."

Never once have I heard Benny speak about the lives

he ended on Dom's orders. Never have I heard regret from him. He doesn't seem to need an answer from me, because he keeps going.

"Dom's gonna pull through this, and once he does, you need to tell him you're out. You're better than this, kid. You don't need this life. It's not for you."

"Then who the hell is it for?" I ask, because I sure as shit don't know.

"Punks like Enzo who don't have anything to lose. You got that woman of yours, and no matter who she really is, she's worth so much more than this."

I cut my gaze to his. "What do you mean, *no matter who she really is?*"

Benny's fingers curl around the paper coffee cup that he still hasn't taken a drink from. "You forget, I spent a lifetime studying people in all sorts of ways. Something ain't right about her."

"Leave it alone, Benny. I have it under control," I tell him, hoping it'll stop him from prying, but it doesn't.

"I saw her eyes, kid. The only reason she'd be covering those up is because she doesn't want anyone to know who she is. Doesn't want anyone to remember her. I told her if she fucked you over, I'd take care of her myself."

My chair is uncomfortable and gets less tolerable by the second. I shift closer to allow our conversation to stay discreet. "Jesus Christ, old man. Don't you dare touch a fucking hair on her head. I know exactly who she is and why she's hiding."

"You sure about that? Because the last woman I saw who had eyes like that was killed in a bloodbath that started a feud that still hasn't ended."

"What the fuck are you talking about?"

He coughs and hacks, finally catching his shallow breath. "It's just a feeling, but my gut has saved my life more than once, and I don't think it's wrong this time either."

I need to know. "What woman?"

Holly and Memphis walk toward us, and Benny goes quiet. Before I can ask him again, a doctor steps into the waiting room.

"Is the Karas family here?"

I jump out of my seat and head for Holly and Memphis. Holly holds out her arm, and I take it. Cav is right behind her.

"Yes," she says. "We're the Karas family. Please, God, tell us he's okay."

CHAPTER
TWENTY-SIX

Holly huddles at Creighton's bedside, where he's slipped in and out of consciousness over the last few hours since he's been out of recovery. A bullet nicked his spleen, but they were able to repair it and his prognosis is excellent.

Thankfully, the ER got Greer stitched up from the shard of flying glass that sliced her arm, and she and Cav just left Creighton's room to give Holly some time alone.

Dom and Enzo are both still in surgery, but we've only gotten updates about Dom. He had a fully blocked artery, and they're working on the bypass and the stent.

Throughout it all, Memphis has been a rock. She's calm, collected, offering a shoulder to cry on to Holly, and making sure Cav and Greer have everything they need. It's like she's already more part of the family than I ever have been, and I'm fucking glad.

Every time she makes another round, going from one person to the next, she stops beside me, curls into my side, and lets me hold her until we're both ready to keep pushing on.

It's closing in on midnight, and the halls of the hospital have quieted. Only nurses in scrubs or patients in gowns walk soundlessly behind us, as if not wanting to disturb our vigil.

"Have they given another update on Dom?" she asks, standing beside me.

I wrap my arm around her shoulders and hug her to my side. "Not yet. I'm hoping he'll be out of surgery anytime."

"Do we need to be worrying?"

I glance down at her troubled tone. "What do you mean?"

She looks in one direction and then the other, double-checking to see if we're truly alone before speaking. "The Rossettis. Are they going to try again? Do we need security here? What about when we leave?"

My brain has been running in the same direction, but I've been deliberately keeping it to myself since we've been in the hospital. "I don't think the Rossettis are bold enough to try to get to us here."

"What about when we leave, though? Eden said something about a hotel, but that doesn't seem like a smart idea."

A janitor pushes a cleaning cart down the hall, and we both wait for him to pass before continuing our conversation. Part of me hates that Memphis is now as aware as I am, but the other part of me is glad. A little paranoia is a good thing when it comes to keeping safe.

"No one's going to a hotel," I tell her with a squeeze to her hand. "It's not secure enough."

She looks tired, and it's clear the night has taken a toll on her. "Then where are they all going to go?"

"Dom's brownstone. It's one of the safest places in the city. Primo and Warren are waiting in SUVs out front, so transport won't be a problem either."

Memphis turns to glance over her shoulder in the direction of the seating area where Eden, Bishop, and the others wait for news. "You think they'll leave here without Dom?"

"They'll do whatever I tell them to."

Her brow furrows with confusion. "They will?"

I nod, about to say words I never expected to admit out loud. "Yeah, because with Dom and Enzo both out of commission, I'm in charge of the Casso family."

CHAPTER TWENTY-SEVEN

MEMPHIS

annon's in charge of the Casso family. I don't know why the realization surprises me, but the shock waves vibrating through my body are from exactly that.

He lets go of my hand as a doctor enters Creighton's room and approaches Holly. "I'm going to listen to what he says, okay?"

I release his hand, knowing that Holly needs him more than I do right now. "Go. I'll be in the waiting room seeing if anyone needs anything. Do what you need to do."

His lips brush over my forehead before he enters Creighton's room and stands behind Holly's chair, his hands on her shoulders. Holly reaches up and squeezes Cannon's hand for support.

Good. After this, I hope like hell Creighton Karas realizes that he's an asshole for pushing Cannon out of his life, especially when there's literally nothing Cannon wouldn't do for him.

I watch them for a few more moments before making my way back to the waiting room. Inside, everyone is starting to droop. Or rather, long past *starting* to droop. Cav sits on a sofa and Greer leans back in his arms, her eyes closed.

I assume that they gave her painkillers for her stitches and they're probably knocking her out. Bishop stands in a corner, where he leans with both arms crossed. Eden stops pacing the room and asks if Greer is okay before she steps out to take yet another walk down the hall to check on her other family members. Benny's asleep with his feet up on a coffee table and a *National Geographic* magazine spread out on his chest.

I barely know these people, but they've already become so very dear to me because I know how much they mean to Cannon. They're the family he desperately wants to be close to, but given his history, he's willing to take whatever he can get. Even if, like from Creighton and Dom, all he can get is scraps.

A flame of anger ignites in me when I think about how they've treated him. *It's not fucking fair.* Right there, in the surgery waiting room of New York Presbyterian, I make a vow.

Every single piece of me that he wants? It's his. I'm not holding anything back. He deserves everything.

"He's awake!" Eden's voice pierces the silence of the waiting room, and we all freeze for a beat before bursting into movement.

Benny jerks and the magazine tumbles to the floor. Cav holds Greer stable so she can't jostle her new sutures.

"Who's awake?" Bishop asks his wife as he pushes off the wall to stand behind her and look through the glass window.

"Creighton! He's holding Holly's hand and talking!"

161

CHAPTER TWENTY-EIGHT

CANNON

"What the hell are you doing here?"

Creighton's deep voice sounds like it's been run through a wood chipper. His throat has to be torn up from being intubated during surgery, but even being flat on his back on a hospital bed doesn't make his disgust at seeing me any easier to handle.

"Crey. Oh my God. Thank God you're talking. You've been coming in and out, and I couldn't get a single straight word out of you." Holly smooths a hand over her husband's pale cheek.

Creighton's gaze fixes on his wife's face, and he curls his fingers around her hand before glaring at me. "What the fuck happened?"

"There was a drive-by shooting," I say, not wanting to say too much because no doubt a doctor or nurse is heading this way.

"Remember, Crey? We were all on the sidewalk, unveiling the car . . ." Holly prompts his memory, and Creighton winces.

"Fuck. The bullets started spraying. I didn't want you to get hit." Even laid up, his protectiveness over his wife is strong. "Are you okay? God, did you get hurt?"

"No. I'm fine," she says, reassuring him to prevent any extra stress. "You should've been worrying about yourself because you're the one who got hit. I've been losing my ever-loving mind since the second I saw that blood on you. Don't you ever do that to me again. *Ever.* Do you hear me, Creighton Karas? I don't care how—"

His expression softens to offer comfort to Holly, who's about to lose it. "Shhh. I'm fine. I promise. I won't get shot again."

"Damn right you're not. I'm not having it. I don't give a damn how much money you have to spend on security. We're not doing this again."

Creighton's gaze cuts to me as Holly buries her face against his chest. "I take it this has to do with Dom?"

"Of course," I tell him, wondering what he's going to do next. Disown the father that worships his every move?

"Where is he?" When Holly lifts her head, some of Creighton's newfound color fades as he studies her face. "Oh fuck."

"He's in surgery," I add quickly, because it's obvious from his reaction he's assuming the worst. "Heart attack. Not a gunshot wound. I swear to Christ he's unkillable. He'll pull through this too."

Creighton attempts to sit up but relents with a slight grimace when he realizes it's not a wise move. "Who else?"

I tell him who's here, waiting to make sure he's all right, and rattle off a few names of others who were gunned down at the party, not that I expect Creighton will know who the other victims are—but we're talking. Something that we haven't done in far too long.

Then a doctor comes into the room, and I back toward the door.

"Mr. Karas, it's a pleasure to see you awake. I'm Dr.—" The doctor starts her spiel as I reach the doorway.

"Cannon. Wait."

When Creighton interrupts the doctor to stop me from leaving, something too close to the feeling of hope rises in my chest.

"Yeah, Crey?"

"I want to talk to you. Alone. Before anyone leaves this fucking hospital."

Slowly, I incline my chin. "Not a problem."

Memphis is waiting just outside with Eden, Bishop, Cav, and Greer.

"Thank God he's awake," Greer whispers. "I don't think I'd know what to do without that bossy, managing bastard trying to control our lives."

The others laugh, but I can't summon even a chuckle. I know exactly what it's like not to have the bossy, managing bastard try to control my life. As great as it sounds, I miss my best friend.

Memphis slides inside the curve of my arm and wraps both of hers around me. "You're going to get your chance to fix this with Creighton. I swear, I'll shoot him myself if he doesn't put this stuff between you in the past."

Glancing down at her, I wish I was staring into her teal-colored eyes instead of the dark brown contacts.

"Is that right?"

She nods. "There isn't much I wouldn't do for you,

Danger. I hope you know that. Whatever you need from me—today, tomorrow, or beyond—I'm here. Just tell me what you need me to do, and I've got it."

I think about the conversation we had about safety and the brownstone. I need to get everyone out of here, except for Holly, because I know there's no way she'll leave Creighton's side. Everyone else needs to be locked down where it's safe.

I text Primo, and a few minutes later, he and one of his brothers cross the lobby to stop in front of me and Memphis.

"Yes, sir?" The respect in his tone is new. He knows the score.

With Dom and Enzo out of commission, I'm the man with the orders. The knowledge solidifies my decisions.

"Give Tempo your keys. He and Warren are taking the entire family back to the brownstone except me, you, and Holly. I've got more security on the way, and we're holding down the fort to watch over Creighton, Dom, and Enzo. Everyone else is kept safe at the brownstone while we work out our next steps."

Tempo's jaw tenses as his brother fishes the keys out of his trouser pockets. "I wish we could retaliate. Won't they come at us again harder if they think we're too weak to hit them back?"

"Dom wouldn't take a chance with his family. They're our first priority. We get them out of here and make sure they're safe. I'll ask for another update on Dom and Enzo before everyone goes."

When Tempo doesn't reply at first, I stare him down to be sure I'm making myself clear. "Do you have a problem carrying out the direct orders you're being given?"

His pale blue eyes take on an icy cast. "No, sir. I'll keep them safe."

I glance over my shoulder to where Memphis stands near Eden. "With your life, if necessary. Got me?"

Tempo gives me a short nod. "Understood, sir."

As the brothers back away, a surgeon enters the waiting room. "Lorenzo Angelini's family?"

No one steps forward, and when it's clear no one plans to, I do.

"Right here."

The surgeon doesn't ask for any further identifying information. "Mr. Angelini is out of surgery and stable. However, he came out of his anesthesia very quickly and is agitated. If you could speak to him and explain that he's not leaving this hospital, you'll save him from getting sedated again right away. We can't take the chance that he's going to tear his stitches. Internal bleeding is a concern."

"Where is he?" Enzo is the least of my worries, but the sooner everyone connected to the Casso family is out of the hospital, the better. You're only as strong as your weakest link, and that's Enzo, as far as I'm concerned.

"Follow me."

Memphis reaches out, and I briefly touch her fingers as I pass and follow the surgeon out of the room to see Enzo.

As soon as we enter, I can tell why the surgeon looks so concerned. Enzo is on his feet, despite the fact that he's weaving from side to side.

"Sit your ass down, Enzo. What the hell do you think you're doing?"

The doctor says, "Please, Mr.—"

"I'm going after those motherfuckers. I'm gonna kill 'em all. No one puts a bullet in me without getting a face full of lead." Enzo rips wires off the leads connected to his chest, and shoves at the nurse trying to stop him. "Get out of my fucking way, bitch."

I stalk toward him. "Sit the fuck down, Enzo. You want to make it through surgery just to die now? Fucking idiot."

Enzo bares his teeth like a wild animal. "*You* can't stop me. Who the fuck do you think you are?"

"Mr. Angelini, you're very upset, we understand. But you're going to cause yourself more injuries if you don't—"

Enzo charges at the nurse and she knocks into the IV pole, sending it crashing to the floor.

"I'm calling security," the doctor shouts, rushing to the panel on the wall.

"Sedate him," I say, offering a hand to the nurse to help her up.

The two hospital employees trade looks, and the doctor nods to the nurse. "Do it. Use restraints if necessary."

Enzo wobbles on his feet, his arms flying out from his sides as he looks for something to keep him upright.

Alarms sound in the room, and footsteps pound down the hall as Enzo drops to the floor and codes.

Great. Just fucking great.

CHAPTER TWENTY-NINE

Enzo isn't dead, but he's lucky as hell.

With the exception of Holly, I gather everyone in a private waiting room to tell them what's happening next.

When I've got everyone's attention, I start. "Until we have identified and neutralized the threat responsible for us all standing in this waiting room, we're all taking precautions."

"What kind of precautions?" Cav asks. "Because if we need extra security, I have an agency we use when we're in the city. They can send us a dozen guys, if necessary."

"Good to know. Right now, I think the safest thing for everyone is to go back to Dom's."

"His brownstone in Hell's Kitchen?" Eden asks. She's surprised I'd suggest our father's version of a castle, a place most of us weren't typically welcomed in growing up.

"Yeah. It's locked down better than any place in the

city. We've got people I trust there, and armored SUVs to transport you."

"What about Banner and Logan?" Greer asks, holding up her phone. "They're checked into a hotel in Jersey. They stashed the car at a garage with a guy Logan knows."

"Tell them to stay put. Actually, tell them to stay the hell out of the city since they're already out safely. We can worry about the car later."

"What do you mean, *since they're already out safely?* Can't we leave safely too?" Greer's voice takes on a panicky undertone.

"You know the game, Greer. We have to be smart. Watch our moves. Whoever shot up the restaurant might not have any problem coming back to finish whatever they were after." This reply comes from Cav.

I'm thankful my half brother gets what's going on. After all, he spent plenty of time growing up in this life, the life I never really wanted. But here I am, handing out orders like I'm Dom himself.

"*Everyone* in this waiting room is going to the brownstone. The club will be closed, but I'll make sure Tanya arranges meals for everyone."

"And then what?" Eden's gaze bounces from me to the bearded, tattooed man beside her. "Because last time I had to go into hiding, I kind of ended up married and didn't come home for a long while."

While Eden and Bishop's story is their own, I get what she's saying.

"It won't be indefinite. Just until we figure out who did this and how we're going to handle them." In the back of my mind, the name *Rossetti* is blaring, and while my instincts are usually pretty damn accurate, I want proof before I go off half-cocked like Enzo. I didn't see them with my own eyes like Benny claimed he did.

Are they the most likely candidates? Absolutely.

Am I going to make the streets run red with the blood of innocents like they did? Absolutely fucking not.

Benny rises from his chair, his magazine tucked under his arm. "I'll help you figure out exactly who needs to pay for this. Get me back to Dom's, and I'll dig up my old Rolodex of contacts and start asking questions."

"Thanks, Benny, but you don't have to get involved. You're retired."

"That's where you're wrong, kid. You don't ever retire in this business. You just get less active. I'm ready. Put me to use."

From beside me, Memphis whispers, "I'm really good at digging. You could say it's my special skill. If there's a laptop I can use at his place, I can get to work. Plus, I have a friend who can pull the camera footage of every shop on the street and get us a video of everything. I should've thought of it sooner. I was just—"

I wrap my arm around her and squeeze tighter. "We've been busy. It's okay. Call in whatever favors you can, *safely*. I'll take all the help I can get."

I look away from her face to the others in the room. It's a strange mix of people, some who understand the situation we're in, and some who just think they do.

"Whoever has connections—call them in. Discreetly."

"What about the cop who was on the scene? Should we be asking him for help?" Greer brings up Clinton Cole's presence right after the shooting happened, and I could kick myself for not thinking of him first.

I reach up and scratch the back of my neck. "I'll talk to him. No matter what happens next, no one else connected to this family gets hurt."

Memphis, Eden, Bishop, Greer, Cav, and Benny left with Warren and Tempo to head to the brownstone. With nothing else to do but wait for another update about Dom, I stand in the doorway to Creighton's room.

Holly sits beside his bed, holding his hand.

"He's out again?" I ask, even though the rhythmic rise and fall of Creighton's chest signal he's asleep once more.

"Yeah. He talked for a bit, but then they gave him some more pain meds and he said he wanted to rest his eyes for a minute. I take that as code for sleeping." A hopeful note underpins Holly's tone, and it bolsters the optimism I'm feeling.

"The doc have anything more to say?"

"Just that he needs to take it easy so his body can fully heal." Her eyes turn glassy, so I pull up a chair beside her.

"He's going to be fine, Holly. You know he's a fighter. Stubborn as hell. He'd never leave you and Rose if he could fight against it."

She reaches out to squeeze the hand on my right knee, and I cover hers with my left. "I know, but I still hate seeing him like this."

Creighton's dark hair resting on the white pillow makes the infamous man almost seem mortal. *Almost.*

"And I'm sure he hates you seeing him like this. He'll be back to normal in no time at all."

"I feel helpless. What am I going to do?" Holly looks up at me, and this time big tears well in her eyes and slip free.

I lean in, wrap an arm around her shoulders, and pull her against me. "You're going to sit here and give him a reason to fight. There's not a damn thing in this world that man wouldn't do for you. If seeing him like this makes you cry even a single tear, he'll be better so damn fast, your head's going to spin."

"I hope you're right, because I don't think I could stand it if . . ."

"He's going to be fine. Better than ever. He'll never leave you."

If I didn't absolutely believe what I was saying, I wouldn't have said it. Thankfully, it does the trick and Holly's shaking shoulders still.

"Thank you, Cannon. I'm sorry that things between you have gone this way. I know it kills him too . . . he's just so damn stubborn and proud."

"I know. We both are. But there's not a thing I wouldn't do to have my best friend back. I never even got to tell him that he's my brother. Dom wouldn't let me." I don't know why I'm confessing this to Holly, but I have to get it out.

"I'm so sorry, Cannon. So sorry you both got caught up in something that wasn't your idea."

Her lack of surprise is exactly as I expected. She's probably known about our shared parentage since moments after Creighton found out.

"I'm not sorry," I tell her, watching Creighton for any

sign of waking, but I see nothing. "I wouldn't take back a single thing I did. It might've been Dom's twisted idea, but it was the most important assignment of my life. I wouldn't be the man I am today, if not for Crey. I owe Dom a thank-you, even if your husband wants my head."

"Not . . . your head . . . exactly." The rough words come from between Creighton's lips.

Holly pops out of her chair. "Oh my God, you're awake again. Thank God." She tangles her fingers with his, and Creighton watches me.

"You should've told me what he made you do. I only fucking cared because you didn't tell me yourself."

A lead weight settles in my stomach, and even though I just said I wouldn't take any of it back, I was wrong. There's one piece I'd take back, and that's the deception.

"You wouldn't have trusted me if I'd told you," I reply.

"You're my brother. I'd trust you with my life."

CHAPTER THIRTY

MEMPHIS

There's an extra laptop in Dom's office. Marta will show you where it is. Tell me if you or your hacker friend find anything.

That's the text I got from Cannon this morning after spending a sleepless night in one of the simple apartments inside Dom's brownstone in Hell's Kitchen, and how I found myself standing inside the office of the most notorious mobster in New York City. A gray-haired woman unlocks a cabinet and reveals a stack of laptop boxes. New laptop boxes. Like they just "fell off a truck" somewhere.

A tiny, instinctive part of me wishes she weren't so efficient, because it's killing the reporter in me not to be able to snoop. Then again, even if she left me alone in here right now, I couldn't talk myself into doing it.

Because the Casso family isn't my target now. No, it's the Rossettis.

No one shoots at people I care about and gets away with it. I'll do whatever I have to do to bring them down and get justice. Luckily, that happens to be something I'm very good at, despite the roadblocks I've run into with my father's case. *I haven't forgotten about you, Dad. I promise.*

"You just need one?" Marta asks, holding out the box.

"One, yes. Thank you," I reply, taking it from her so she can relock the cabinet.

"I really hope he knows what he's doing," she adds, and I'm caught off guard.

"What do you mean?"

She turns around and gestures to the door. I take one step but wait for an answer.

"I mean that I hope Cannon knows how to step into the shoes he's trying to fill, and understands the consequences that are going to go along with it. This isn't a road he can untravel. I don't think he fully appreciates what he's taking over."

"Cannon's an intelligent, thoughtful, and incredible man. I'm sure he knows exactly what he's doing and will have no problem filling any role that comes his way."

Her head jerks back like she's stunned to hear me defend him, and it pisses me off a little that Cannon being defended is such a shocking thing.

"Well, apparently you know exactly what you think about the situation, don't you?" she asks me with a dash of attitude creeping into her tone.

"I know Cannon. That's all that matters."

"Hmm. I guess we'll see." She takes her seat at the desk just outside the office door she relocked behind me.

I make my way back out into the lobby to take the stairs down to the apartment one of Dom's guys showed me to in the early hours of the morning. When I'm alone again, I open the laptop.

It's time to get started.

Four hours later, I still haven't heard from Ariel, which isn't surprising since my super-hacker friend has a brand-new baby. So I rise and stretch before heading to the main living quarters in the brownstone where Eden and Bishop are staying. Delicious smells come from the kitchen, and I follow my nose toward the food.

Inside, I'm startled to find Tanya unloading aluminum trays of food on the counter.

"What are you doing here?" I ask.

She twists around to face me, equally shocked to see me as I was to see her. "I should be asking you that, but then again, it doesn't surprise me to find you locked down with the family. Cannon's made how he feels about you pretty clear."

"What do you mean?" I ask, mostly because I didn't expect her to know much of anything when it comes to how Cannon feels about me.

"He called me last night to tell me the club was closing indefinitely, and that you weren't going to be working there until it was safe. He said he wasn't taking any chances with anything, especially you."

Warmth bubbles up in my chest, and I want to wrap my arms around her statement and hold on to it until I see Cannon next and can hug him.

"He had you bring over food?"

Tanya gives me a quick nod. "Yeah. He wanted to make sure everyone has everything they need." She pauses in unclamping the lid of one container and bites her lip. "Is it true that Enzo almost died? Cannon didn't say much, and the gossip mill is hard at work."

I can't help but wonder what the motivation is behind her question. "Do you have some special interest in Enzo?"

Tanya's head whips back and forth. "No. Total opposite. He's awful. And I know I shouldn't say this, but if that's not true, I wish it was." Something that looks a lot like fear lines her features.

"What did he do to you?"

Tanya's expression turns wary. "Why do you always ask so many questions?"

Part of me wants to laugh, because she has no idea how good I am at getting information out of people. I lift my chin and stare Tanya down.

"You brought up Enzo, not me. You're also the one who basically just said you wish he was dead. Wouldn't you be curious too if you were me, Tanya?"

She huffs, but I can tell I made my point. "He made a play for Teal after he saw her at the club. Cannon had to warn him off. Enzo didn't listen, so Cannon made him."

Of course he did. Because that's what Cannon does. Save everyone. *But who's going to save him?*

"How did Cannon make him listen?" I ask, wondering if that explains more of the bad blood between Cannon and Enzo, or if it comes from something else.

"Beat the hell out of him. After that, I heard Enzo tried to make Dom throw Cannon out because of it, but Dom put his foot down. Said no one tells him how to run his organization, and no one got to touch a woman against her will without consequences."

The older man I once wanted to see rotting in prison continues to surprise me with his defense of women and his unwillingness to let violence rule his crew when he easily could.

"What do you know about the Rossettis?" I ask. "Because that's who Cannon thinks did this."

Tanya's expression turns hard. "They're no good. GTR sniffed around Teal too. She's a magnet for bad seeds. He scares me even more than Enzo does, if you want to know the truth. There's something not right about him. That's another reason why Cannon had to pull Teal off working the nights we had meetings. On top of all her other issues, she attracted too much attention." Tanya's lips tilt to one side as she pauses to consider me. "And then he just made it worse by bringing you in and getting everyone riled up over you."

"Who brought food? This smells a hell of a lot better than those bagels and lox Dumb and Dumber tried to get us to eat this morning." Benny's voice comes from the doorway of the kitchen as he follows his nose, much the same way I did.

"Benny, it's been a long time," Tanya says, stepping toward the old man to hug him.

"Hey, gorgeous, they finally let you out of that club?"

She grins and kisses his cheek.

The old gangster adds, "It's about time. You gonna finally run away with me? Leave it all behind for the Florida sunshine?"

Clearly, the older man knows Tanya well. I have to

assume that he was probably a cigar smoker at the club for years, which could explain the coughing fits and the blood smear on his handkerchief. One of our network execs had lung cancer, and I remember him doing the same thing. I have to wonder what Benny's dealing with, because I have a feeling it's not good.

"All you have to do is say the word, and I'll leave this city behind, Benny."

"Where's your sister? How's she doing these days?"

Tanya shoots me a look and bites her lip. "Hopefully, she's in the right place to get better now, Ben. It's a process."

One side of his mouth pinches to the side. "Ah, man, her demons finally caught up with her?"

"Something like that. But she's gonna be good as new once she's done with rehab."

"Pretty girl. She just needs to realize that's not all she has to offer the world," Benny says before stepping toward the aluminum trays. "Now, what's for lunch?"

Instead of heading back to the apartment with my food, I stay in the common area and eat with the others. I've always been a loner, but with them, it's easy to talk and laugh and generally distract ourselves from everything going on.

Then the conversation turns to more serious things.

"How long are you staying?" Bishop asks Cav, after telling us that he booked a flight for the next day for himself and Eden. They're taking no chances getting back to New Orleans safe and sound.

Greer leans against Cav. "I'm not leaving until Crey is released, but I can't imagine he'll want to stay long, though. If I know my brother, he'll want to get back to baby Rose as quickly as possible."

"I don't want to run," Cav says, directing his comment to his wife. "But I'll get you the hell out of here as fast as I can. I'm not taking any fucking chances with you either. One set of stitches is enough."

My hand tightens on the laptop beside me. Now more than ever, I need to get back to my digging. There's just one thing I can't figure out.

"Benny, do you know what started the feud between the Cassos and the Rossettis? Cannon never told me."

The older man looks up from a bowl of ice cream heavily laden with chocolate syrup. "The feud that'll never die? I'm not sure anyone wants to talk about why it started. They're just interested in finishing it."

"But you were around when it started? Working for Dom?"

His spoon clinks against the bowl as he dives in for another bite. At this rate, the entire serving will be gone in less than five scoops. "It's not something we talk about. Those were dark days."

His reply tells me, more than ever, that the cause is something I need to know.

"Dark days like when I had to run for it?" Eden asks, peering into the kitchen around Bishop's shoulder.

Benny's attention cuts to her, and he smiles like someone who just caught a glimpse of their favorite grandkid. I wonder if that's how Benny feels about everyone either in this building or laid up inside the hospital—that they're *family.* Maybe it's cold-blooded of me to think that's a positive thing that I can use to find answers, but I don't care. Right now, anything that stops more bullets from flying is worth the cost.

"Darker, kid. That's why we don't talk about it." Benny drops the spoon in his bowl with a clank of metal on ceramic, shuffles to the sink to dump it out, and rinses it with hot water.

Dark enough that it puts Benny off his ice cream? Yep, definitely something there.

"I'll catch all of you later. This old man needs a nap." He moves out of the kitchen, and everyone watches him silently.

It takes one round of glances bouncing from person to person in the room for me to make a decision.

"I'm going after him," I say to no one in particular, or maybe to everyone. Since there are no objections, I rush out of the room to catch Benny on the stairs, heading in a direction I haven't yet ventured.

"Benny . . ." When I say his name, the old man waves me off.

"Not now. I'm tired."

He takes another turn, and I stay on his heels down the hallway.

"You're not tired. You're dying." My assumption is out of my mouth before I realize what I'm saying.

Benny spins around to face me, his expression the opposite of friendly. "You think you're some hotshot detective figuring that out? What the hell do you want, Drew Carson?"

My gut, which has guided me faithfully my entire life, tells me that I have to give him some of the truth if he's going to trust me with anything.

"I want to find a way to fix this without any more blood being spilled. I didn't find Cannon now just to lose him to some mob war I don't understand, and no one knows how it started. I need answers so I can try to save this family, because I desperately want it to be mine too."

Every word out of my mouth is the absolute truth, and from the way Benny studies me, he sees it too.

"You got it bad, kid. Not that I'm surprised. Cannon's a good one. Maybe the best of all of them. You'd do right to grab onto him and convince him to get the hell out of this mess before a bullet with his name on it finds its mark."

"I wish it was that easy. But you know him. Better than me, no doubt. And that means you know that he's not going to walk away when the people he loves are in danger. Not a chance."

Benny rocks back on his heels. "Yeah, because he's got a heart of gold, and not even fool's gold at that." As soon as I think he's being swayed in my favor, Benny turns and continues on down the hallway.

"Dammit," I whisper to myself, feeling like I've lost an important battle, but I'm not even sure why I feel that way.

The events of the past twenty-four hours crash down on me, all the highs and lows and craziness. My lack of proper sleep weighs on my shoulders, causing me to slump against a doorway. But I force my exhaustion down and dig deep for a second wind.

"You coming or what, Drew Carson?" Benny waits at the end of the hallway, his hand resting on a doorway.

"Coming for what?"

"Your answers. I ain't got all day."

CHAPTER THIRTY-ONE

CANNON

"I need to get out of this fucking bed. I got work to do."

My father is just as stubborn as Enzo, which shouldn't come as a surprise, although I expected he'd be a little smarter.

"You're not getting discharged for at least another forty-eight hours. You just had major surgery," I tell him as he rips one lead from his chest.

"Then I'll go against medical advice. I don't fucking care. I'm not going to let them take everything I've built. Not now. Not after all these years."

A nurse comes jogging into the room as soon as she sees what Dom's doing, and Primo takes a step toward Dom. I raise my hand to indicate the bodyguard needs to stay put.

"Sir, please. You need to stay in bed and leave the monitoring equipment alone. It's for your own safety," the nurse says, her calm tone edged with *mild* authority. No doubt because she knows exactly who this man is.

He's gotten the royal treatment due to his infamy, much like Creighton has. The hospital staff has gone above and beyond to make sure every need is met before we even have to ask. They'll definitely be getting a large anonymous donation soon.

"If I want to leave, I'll leave. No one's stopping me."

Instead of shrinking at Dom's authoritative tone, she lifts her chin and her posture stiffens.

"Sir, with all due respect, the surgeons didn't just spend hours of their precious time saving your life when they could've been working on someone more grateful, just so you could undo all of their work and throw it back in their faces. If you walk out of this hospital, I wouldn't be surprised if you drop dead on the sidewalk before you make it to your car. And even if you don't drop dead, but simply pass out or need a second surgery, there's a chance those same surgeons might not be quite so quick to rush to your rescue." Her gaze shoots at me, and instead of seeing latent fear pushing its way out, her gray eyes are flinty. "We don't appreciate people who don't give a damn about their health and waste our time in the process."

I don't know what it is about her or her statement, but Dom's hand stills and he leaves the other lead on his chest.

"No one talks to me that way. Ever."

The brazen nurse pins her shoulders back and stares my father down. "Well, you can make a note in your diary that today, Judith Maria Hansen is speaking to you *that way*, and if you've got enough brain cells left in that hard head of yours, you'll listen to what I'm saying. You need to take it easy and keep your blood pressure down. Now, if you'll allow me, I'll reaffix the lead and you can continue your discussion."

Dom says nothing, but she doesn't need words from him. Bold as you please, she steps right up to the bed and picks up the discarded lead and sticks it back to his chest.

"Now, Mr. Casso, can I get you anything? Water? A magazine?"

Dom's gaze lifts to hers, and unexpectedly, a chuckle falls from his lips as his chest bounces. "You've got balls, Judith Maria Hansen. Big, brass ones that should clank when you walk through the hallways and make it damn near impossible to do your job."

"Thank you, sir. I'll take that as a compliment. If you want anything, please don't hesitate to ring. I'm on call for the next ten hours, and you'll be seeing me a lot. Even if I have to hunt you down." With that final threat, she backs out of the room with a nod to Primo and disappears down the hall.

Dom watches her closely as she leaves. "Damn. What a fucking woman, am I right? I'm gonna have to get her number before I get the hell out of this place."

I didn't look at Nurse Judith with anything but an eye toward information, but now that she's out of sight, her appearance sinks in. She looked to be around fifty, fit, trim, and pretty with short dark hair and librarian-style glasses. Also, completely not Dom's type, as he usually goes after women in their late twenties and thirties who have daddy issues and are drawn to his power, but are definitely scared of him.

Judith is none of those things.

Which makes her all the more intriguing, especially if

Dom's staring after her with a wonderstruck expression I've never seen on his face.

Then, like he flipped a switch, his features morph into a calculating look as his attention snaps back to me.

"Where the hell is Enzo? If I'm out of commission, someone needs to handle things and fast. He'll know what to do. Who to call. Who to fucking kill. Paulie and Junior will have his back, and this will all be over fast."

Enzo. That's who he wants to handle shit. *Of course.* Still doesn't fucking matter, because he's back in surgery after his stupid little stunt. Which probably explains why Judith was so adamant that Dom take it easy.

And *fuck.* I haven't even had a chance to tell him about Paulie and Junior not pulling through. Given what Judith just said about Dom's blood pressure, now isn't the best time to give him any of that information. At least, nothing but the basics.

"Enzo's out of commission. He took a bullet and they're still working on him."

Dom's heart rate kicks up on the monitoring equipment, and I know that's the extent of what I can safely tell him.

"What the fuck do you mean? Is he going to be okay?"

I don't have a single fucking clue, but I take a page out of Dom's book and lie to him. "He's going to be fine. He'll need a lot of rest and recuperation time, just like you."

"Goddammit. Then get the others in here. I need to lay out a plan that even they can't fuck up."

I pull up the chair to his bedside and take a seat. The next words out of my mouth may change the course of my life forever, but I truly feel I have no choice. It's time for me to step up and take my place. I'm done living on the fringes, leaving the safety of my family to chance.

For the first time in my life, I tell Dom how things are going to go, and there's nothing he can do about it. "Whatever plan you've got, you tell me and I'll handle it."

Dom stares at me like I just told him I've been convicted of murder in seventeen states.

"What the fuck? You're no gangster. You don't know the first thing about how the fuck to retaliate after an event like this. You think you can go spray bullets and take them out?"

I stare down my father with even more confidence than I saw on Judith's face. "You're right. I'm no fucking gangster, but it's about time this family stops writing its history with blood on the streets. We're better than that."

Dom jerks his head back, but the stack of pillows stops it from moving much. "And what fucking way do you think you're going to make things happen? By talking? Those sons of bitches will kill you as soon as they see you. You're my worst-kept fucking secret."

My resolve hardens, and I refuse to let the caustic tone of his words affect me. Dom may be my father, but he's never been a dad. Those are two separate fucking things.

Pushing back the chair, I rise and loom over his bedside. "You're flat on your back. Your men are out of commission. I might be your worst-kept fucking secret, but I'm the one who's finally going to take care of the shit you've let hang over this family for years."

I back away toward the door as Dom's stare turns harder with my every step. I grip the doorway.

"You don't think I can do it? That's fine by me, Dom. I'll let you know when it's done. You can thank me then."

I stride out of the room and stalk down the hall.

"Cannon."

My name comes out of nowhere, and my head's on a swivel as I try to figure out where the hell the rough voice is coming from. The room next door belongs to Creighton, and he's sitting up in his bed with Holly nowhere in sight.

I stop in the doorway. "What?"

He's propped up on pillows, and I'm happy to see his color has started to come back. Of course a bullet wouldn't be able to keep Creighton Karas down for long. The man's practically superhuman.

He waves me in with two fingers, and like the errand boy I've always been, I step inside at his beckoning. As soon as the thought occurs to me, my feet stop when I'm only halfway to his bed.

"What?" I repeat, my tone sharp.

Creighton swallows, and I'm reminded of all the times I picked up the phone to reach out to him for advice, but didn't call because he told me he never wanted to hear from me again.

"You've got nothing to prove to that old man or anyone else. You hear me?"

My hands clench into fists at my sides. "It's been years, Crey. You don't know shit about me anymore, including what I've got to prove and to whom."

"It hasn't been long enough for me to forget what kind of man you are. You want to get out of this shit? This life?

I can get you out. Cut ties with Dom. Walk away and move on."

The muscle in his jaw ticks, and I have to wonder if he's holding himself back from straight up giving me orders like he used to be able to. But not anymore. I'm not Creighton Karas's man. I'm not anyone's fucking man but *mine.* It's time to prove that to every single goddamned person in the world who thinks I'm nothing but a lackey.

"I appreciate your offer, Crey. But I don't need it. I'm done following Dom's orders or anyone else's. I'm my own man, and I make my own fucking decisions."

Creighton's lined features smooth out. His dark gaze shifts, and what I see there looks a hell of a lot like pride.

"Be safe then, brother. You and I have a lot to talk about when I get out of here, and I'll regret it until the last day of my life if we don't get that chance."

Brother.

The word hits me like a cement truck.

This man, the one who helped me figure out exactly who I was and taught me so much about life, is recognizing me as an equal. The weight I've been carrying around at the breach in our relationship dissipates where I stand.

"I'd like that, Crey. See you soon."

He nods at me and I head out of the room, almost running into Holly, who is returning with a container from the cafeteria.

"Holly. Take care of him."

"I will, Cannon." She smiles at me. "And you take care of yourself."

I stride out of the room, sure she overheard at least

part of our brief conversation. I'm almost to the next doorway when I hear Creighton's gravelly voice, and my feet stop of their own volition.

"He better not get himself killed. Not now. Not when I'm just getting him back. I won't have it."

"Oh, babe. You know Cannon's not like that."

"That was before. I don't know this Cannon, but I sure as hell hope I get the chance to."

I don't know if Creighton is aware I can still hear him, but I start moving again, my determination fueled by sources in every direction.

Memphis. Dom. Creighton and Holly. Enzo. Paulie and Junior. The rest of the family. Everyone we've lost and everyone who still needs saving.

Their lives are in my hands, and it's not a responsibility I take lightly.

CHAPTER
THIRTY-TWO

Benny shoos me out of the room the second after he puts the thick leather-bound journal in my hand. The only thing he says is, "The names have been changed, but the story's there. Don't tell anyone I gave this to you, especially not Dom. Now leave me the hell alone."

I stroll away from the library with the book tucked under my arm like contraband, waiting until I close the door to my small apartment to yank it out and flip open the cover. On the first page is a handwritten title.

Tales from the Inside:
A Former Mobster's Memories

Holy. Fuck.

Is this what I think it is?

I'm half-terrified for Benny, but also half-terrified to *hope* that this is a mob memoir that covers the feud between the Cassos and the Rossettis.

Was Benny going to publish this? Maybe as his last offering to the world before he dies?

I don't know what to think, but that can wait. Right now, I have some major reading to do.

I get lost in the words and pictures inside the leather journal. I'm almost halfway through the book, and when I look up and blink, the clock has ticked past two hours.

Two hours? Jesus. How is that even possible?

Oh, right. I've been engrossed in a hit man's chronicles of mob history.

As for what I've learned about the two families—they were never friends. They were always enemies. According to the handwritten story, Benny thinks the feud began back in the days of Prohibition when both sides were selling bootleg spirits up and down the five boroughs, trying to keep the population of New York well-liquored so the families could rake in as much cash as possible. They lived like kings, with the best of everything, but it was all too often ripped away by the cops who weren't on their payrolls and judges who despised their autonomy.

Each family did everything they could to throw the other under the bus. At least until the world went to war. Everything changed as men who used to shoot at their own countrymen turned their sights on others. When they came back, nothing was ever the same.

Prohibition was over, and they had to find a new way to make money. Woven in with tales of World War II were the rising and falling tides of the mob and the families that scrambled for power, dodging the law every chance they could get.

It read more like an adventure novel in some parts, filled with glittering highs and devastating lows. And then eventually, a new breed of mobster climbed the ranks. Although the names have been changed as well as the descriptions, I have a sneaking suspicion I'm reading about Dom Casso and his rise to power.

Smart, strategic, and ruthless when necessary, he was unstoppable. His father before him didn't have nearly the drive, ambition, or vision that Dom had when he took over as the youngest leader of one of the leading mob families.

I stretch my neck from side to side because it has a crick in it from the way I've been sitting, and my shoulders ache. I rise to move around and get my blood flowing again, setting the book down for only a moment, and my phone buzzes in my pocket.

My first thought is *Cannon*, and I yank the phone out.

But it's not him.

RANDI: I heard what happened. Oh my God, are you okay??

I stare down at the screen wondering, first, how the hell she found out what happened. Second, I wonder if she really cares or if she's pumping me for information for GTR Rossetti.

I don't want to believe the second possibility could be true, because that means they're trying to find out what's going on so they can strike at us again.

Us.

I freeze when I realize the word I used. I've just silently declared myself a member of the Casso clan, the very crew I vowed I'd see thrown in prison for the rest of their lives.

But they're not just mobsters to me anymore. Not at all. They're real people with lives and loves, and whether or not it's against my will and better judgment, I care about them. Even Dom, sometimes, when I don't want to whack him upside the head for treating Cannon like crap.

I'm not about to throw them to the Rossettis.

Not sure what I want to say, I tap my thumbs on either side of my phone screen and consider.

If Randi's with the Rossettis, I can use her.

I feel a pang of guilt at the idea of manipulating her, but I don't see that I have much of a choice. Those people shot automatic weapons at a crowd that also included innocents, and hit people who didn't deserve their animosity. They also could have easily killed or injured bystanders.

If nothing else, GTR Rossetti and his father need to be taken off the streets. I don't care that I learned the Cassos are partly good and don't all need to go to prison. I don't feel nearly so kindly about the Rossettis.

I hesitate a few more moments before forming the reply I tap onto the screen.

ME: I'm okay. How did you find out what happened?
RANDI: There was a story on the news last night about a drive-by shooting in Little Italy. I went to the club to find you, but it was closed. That's how I knew the Cassos had to be involved.

Hmm . . . yeah. I don't buy it.

ME: I can't really tell you anything. Just . . . stay away from the club. Stay safe.
RANDI: You're scaring me, Drew. If you need help, I can get you some. I don't know what you're wrapped up with, but if you want out of this mess, I'm here.

What. The. Hell? She should talk.

ME: I'm fine. Thanks.

As soon as I reply to Randi, I can't help but wonder what she thinks is going down, and my suspicions go wild after hours of reading mob stories. She could be working for the Rossettis and trying to draw me out so they can use me as bait.

I drop back into the chair where I've been parked all afternoon and think through it. *I'm not jumping to conclusions because I've spent hours wrapped up in Benny's words. I'm not. But something is definitely going on with Randi's message.*

I need to text Cannon, but I have no idea what he's doing and I'm hesitant to interrupt him. Still, he needs to know about Randi. Plus, I desperately want an update about how things are going and if there's anything he needs.

Deciding a text is the least intrusive way to get to him, I type out a message.

Me: I know you're probably busy, but is there anything I can do to help? I'm here, and I can take on anything you need. Call me when you get a chance. I have something I want to run by you.

CHAPTER THIRTY-THREE

CANNON

I never expected to be at my desk at the club with this man sitting across from me. A man who has never set foot inside here before, and likely will never get another invitation.

"Give me one good reason I shouldn't take you in right now and keep you locked down for questioning for the next twenty-four hours." Clinton Cole's suspicious expression tells me he's smarter than he lets on.

"Because you've got no grounds to hold me. I'm a witness to a crime who invited you here. You should be thanking me, not threatening to arrest me."

"Then what the hell do you have to tell me? What the fuck happened?"

"You were there, Cole. You saw it all go down. You tell me what the fuck happened." When I flip the question around, he glares at me.

"You really don't fucking expect me to tell you anything, do you? Because that's not how this shit works."

"Did you find the car? The driver? Gunman? Anything?"

Cole shifts in his seat, and his stiff posture expresses his annoyance. "You think you're a cop now? You're barely on the right side of the law, Freeman. Why should I tell you shit?"

"Because you're tired of blood being spilled on your watch. Despite being a hard-ass, you're actually a decent cop. I want to end this, and I need your help."

Cole tips back the chair to balance on two feet. "You want to fucking end this, and you want my help?" He swings his head from side to side. "Did I walk into the twilight zone instead of some fancy club?"

"No. But you can't tell me you don't want this over. You want to get the arrest and have your press conference where your boss calls you a hero, and then you have a chance to say you're just doing your job and don't want any recognition for something like that."

With his eyes narrowed, Cole sits the chair back on all its legs. "You think you have me figured out, don't you?"

"I'm working on it."

"Then work on this—I'm not giving you a license to kill. You're not James Bond or Batman. You want to end this shit with the Rossettis, then you turn over everything you have to me, and I'll get with the DA and we put together a case that's airtight and we take them down."

I study him, weighing my next words before they come out of my mouth. "What happens if I agree to do it your way and no one goes down? What if bullets keep flying and take out someone else who matters to me? What then?"

"You know I can't make you any promises, Freeman. That's not how this works. So either get with the program or stop wasting my time. I got better shit to do."

He says that, but I'm willing to put money on the fact that my offer to help is the best option he's got.

"Did you get any surveillance photos of the car? You had to have gotten something, Cole. I know you were out there taking pictures of all of us coming and going."

Cole crosses his arms over his chest, and that movement alone gives me all the answers I need. His statement confirms it.

"So what if I did?"

"Give me the license plate number, and I'll dig up something decent to share with you."

A harsh laugh escapes his lips. "Right, like I believe that shit for a minute."

"I find the car, you go in and arrest the driver. How about that for a deal?"

Cole leans forward, his elbows on the edge of my desk, and speaks low and clear. "Car was found this morning, burned out under a bridge. It's in the crime lab now, but I'm willing to bet my badge on the fact that there won't be shit to find. No fingerprints. No DNA. Registration linked back to a shell corporation propped up by a bunch of dummy names."

The dead end pisses me off, but I'm not going to show any reaction. At least now he's sharing information with me.

"But you've got something else, don't you? Another lead?"

"If I did, why would I tell you and risk getting kicked off the force?"

"Because I'm the best shot you have at ending all of this without spilling another drop of blood. You want my help, it comes with strings attached. Lots of fucking strings."

"I don't like strings, Freeman. If you're serious about taking down the Rossettis without more bloodshed, then you need to drop 'em."

"I'm not dropping shit until I know you're on board. You want to hand an airtight case to the DA, I have all the information you need. And you're right, I'm not fucking Batman, and I'm not going to deliver them all tied up next to a light on top of police headquarters with the bat signal, so that means you gotta walk in there and arrest them without getting killed."

Cole kicks back in his chair, his arms crossed. "What if I don't need you for an airtight case. What if I've already got someone on the inside who can give me what I need to get the DA to sign off."

I sit up straighter, because that's information I didn't have before. But if Cole had everything he needed, he'd already have Giancarlo Rossetti and GTR in jail, awaiting trial. So he might have someone, but they don't have enough information yet.

The real question, though—who the fuck do they have on the inside? I run through every man on the Rossetti roster that I can think of, and most have been in place for years. Dom and Enzo would know more about the newest guys, but I'm not involving them.

"You know you want to ask me who I've got," Cole says, reading my mind.

"You're not going to tell me, so what's the point of wasting my breath? Now, are we doing this, Cole? Or am I handling it myself and you're going to have to explain to your lieutenant why you're not doing your goddamned job?"

Cole glares at me. "What's your fucking plan, Freeman? Tell me, and then we'll make a deal."

CHAPTER
THIRTY-FOUR

Hours later, a text makes my phone vibrate, and I scramble to grab it.

Not Cannon. Dammit.

I read the message from Eden saying dinner has arrived, and I'd better come get it before the guys eat everything.

I'm in the middle of reading about a grisly face-off between two mob bosses over the death of the wife of Sonny Mazzini. Mazzini, who I have to believe is Gianni Rossetti, the former head of the Rossetti family who was succeeded twenty-five years ago by his brother Giancarlo, the father of the notorious GTR.

I leave the journal open, the silk ribbon between the pages, even though I desperately want to keep reading. But even more so, I'm hoping Cannon has come back too.

Spending hours reading about the things these brutal mobsters are capable of makes it even more clear that he is nothing like them. This is something I already knew, but the reading has reinforced it times a billion. Cannon may be the son of Dominic Casso, Marco Ferrari in the book, but there is no way he could do the things that Dom has done.

But what if Dom retires and Cannon decides to take over the family? What then? Would I stand by his side while he ordered the murders of people who had done terrible things?

I love him. That's not in doubt. But would I still love him if he changed so drastically and became remolded in his father's image?

My emotions are strung out, and that's why I have to walk away from the book. Why I have to walk away from this empty little apartment where there's nothing but me and my thoughts.

I need to see Cannon again. I need to reaffirm that he's the man I know and love. The one who bought a building because an old man and his pizza shop were going to be evicted. The man who found out that I was investigating him and his entire family, and rather than rat me out to his father, he promised to find a way for me to get justice for mine while still being able to have *him*.

To say I'm a bit of a wreck right now is the understatement of the century. And when I add my concerns about Cannon taking it upon himself to end this feud that has turned into an all-out war, I just need to fucking *see him*.

I make my way down to the communal kitchen, where Tanya is accompanied by Grice. The pair pull container after container of food out of the oven and set them on the table where Eden, Bishop, Greer, Cav, and Benny are devouring salads and cold appetizers.

"Is Cannon coming back? Has anyone heard from him?" I ask as soon as I stop in the doorway, feeling defeated that he isn't here to greet me.

I just want to see him. Touch him. Talk to him.

"He might be at the club," Tanya says, glancing at me.

"Why would he go there if it's closed?" When Tanya doesn't have a response, I look around the room, hoping anyone else might have an answer for me.

Grice is the one who replies. "It's empty. Perfect for having a meeting with someone you can't be seen with in public."

"Like who?"

"Like the cops." This comes from Benny as he leans back in his chair and laces his fingers together behind his head. "Because Cannon ain't his old man, and there's no way in hell that boy is going to go after the Rossettis with guns blazing like Enzo would if he were stepping in for Dom."

At first I think Benny's being critical of Cannon and I want to jump to his defense, but then he adds, "He's a hell of a lot smarter than Enzo, so he's going to handle this carefully. Like he's walking around with a live bomb, because that's basically what the situation is—ready to fucking explode with one wrong move."

The relief I feel from Benny's statement drains away just as quickly as it appeared.

"The Rossettis don't screw around," Cav says, his tone grave. "They have no problem killing innocents to get what they want. I've seen it before."

"I hate that this is happening," Eden says, visibly shuddering in her seat. Bishop reaches out to wrap a tattooed arm around her, pulling Eden and her chair closer to his massive frame.

"We're on the first flight out of here tomorrow. This will all be a bad dream when we get back to NOLA, cupcake."

Hearing the giant of a man call the petite woman *cupcake* might be the most adorable thing I've ever heard, but Benny interrupts.

"You're leaving before your pop's even out of the hospital? Really? That's harsh, Eden. Real harsh."

Bishop glares at Benny. "Don't try to get in her head, old man. Dom would want her safe, and you know it." His stare touches all of us as he looks around the room. "Dom would want all of you to be safe. When Cannon surfaces, I'm telling him we're leaving. The rest of you can do what you want. Getting Eden out of here is all I care about."

He presses a kiss to her forehead, and a wave of warmth washes over me at his protectiveness. *I love that she has that, and I know Cannon would do the same for me.*

"I agree—you two should go. I'm not leaving until Crey is out of the hospital, though, so let's eat and wait for Cannon. Then we'll make decisions about how the next twenty-four hours will go," Greer says, and we all help ourselves to the food.

Thankfully, Cannon arrives as we're cleaning up.

I bolt away from the table I was just wiping down and run to him, practically throwing myself into his body. "You're back. Thank God."

His strong, capable arms wrap around me and lift me off my feet. "You'd think I'd been off to war with that kind of greeting." He presses a kiss to my lips. "I love it."

"Are you okay? What happened? What's going on? Did you talk to the cops?"

As soon as the word *cops* is out of my mouth, Cannon stiffens.

"What about the cops? Have they been here?"

I shake my head. "No, but Benny thought you might be meeting them at the club."

Cannon puts me on my feet and turns to face the old man, who's still sitting at the table with a chunk of garlic bread on his plate.

"What the fuck, Benny? What do you know that I don't?"

The older man tilts his head to one side and stares down Cannon. "Probably know you better than you know yourself. You ain't no mobster. You don't do wet work. You're not walking up to Giancarlo's door and putting a bullet in his head. I know you, kid. You're working on a plan that keeps your hands clean and takes care of business at the same time."

"Is he right?" I ask, hope coloring my tone.

Cannon's gaze cuts from Benny to me and back again. "I'm looking at all our options."

"How's Dom?" Grice asks from the sink where he and Tanya are doing dishes. I offered, but the two seemed to work better as a team.

"Recovering. He has to keep his stress level low. No getting worked up over anything, which means that *no matter what you fucking hear, you tell him nothing.*" Cannon's gaze travels from one person in the room to the next. "Does everyone in this room hear me? Because if I find out that someone leaked information to him before this is done, whatever happens to Dom is on *your* head."

Everyone murmurs in somber agreement except Cav. He chuckles from the doorway where Greer leans against him.

"What?" Cannon snaps at his half brother.

"You sound like the old man. Probably more than you ever have before. So, big brother, you going to fill us in on what the fuck is going on? Because I'm down to help. Whatever you need."

Greer whips her head around to look at her husband, a protest clearly dying to jump from her lips. But when she sees his face, she only says, "Are you sure about this? Because you're not Dom's errand boy anymore, and you have a hell of a lot to lose now."

"I've still got Casso blood running through my veins, and I'm not going to let those fucking Rossettis gun down another person we care about. They fucking shot at you. My sister. My brothers. My family. I can't let that go."

Like Greer finally sees the toll it's taken on the love of her life, she begins to comfort him. "Cav—"

"We're not killing anyone," Cannon says. "I did meet with the cops. Well, one cop. Clinton Cole."

"So, what's the plan?" Benny asks.

"We need every single thing Dom has on them. Pictures. Wiretaps. Evidence. Every goddamned thing. We're putting together a case for the DA that's airtight."

"And you really think that shit is going to stick?" Benny says.

Cannon pulls me tighter against his side. "He's also got

a man on the inside, and together with whatever they've got, we're taking down the whole fucking Rossetti family."

CHAPTER THIRTY-FIVE

CANNON

I can tell Benny's skeptical about my plan, but I don't fucking care. It's not his decision. Before I leave the kitchen, I extract a promise from him that he won't go to Dom to tell him anything. Making him swear on the life of his granddaughter might be a little extreme, but my mob roots are showing.

If Dom got word of what I was planning, there's no way in hell he'd let it happen. Cooperating with the cops, especially bringing one into the club, is probably enough to get him to shoot me in the damn head, but I don't care. Like I told him, I'm handling this my way.

But before I ransack Dom's office to find everything he has on the Rossettis and deliver it to Cole, I need some time with Memphis. *Alone.* I didn't see her text until I was on my way here, and decided that it would be easier to tell her everything in person. Because she's *my* person.

Memphis is the reason I'm doing all of this. She has no idea that if she hadn't walked into my life, I might be taking a different path right now. You don't grow up in the mob without knowing what you're capable of, and if I had to step into Dom's shoes to mete out justice for the insult that they served us—especially if they'd killed my friends and family and not just wounded them—I could do it.

Dom may not realize it, but my brain works a hell of a lot like his. I can pretty much imagine exactly what he wants to do right now, and I'm not going to let it happen. The potential for collateral damage is too high.

I'm not letting this feud take another life of someone I love.

I link my fingers with Memphis's as I follow her up to the tiny apartment that she crashed in without me last night. There's a whole hell of a lot I would have given to be wrapped around her, but duty called, and I couldn't leave Holly alone while Creighton was unconscious. Even though he'd cut me out, my loyalty doesn't end like that. Once a brother, always a brother.

Just like now that this woman is mine, she always will be. *No matter what.*

As soon as she shuts the door behind us, the off-white walls and tan-and-brown carpet fade away, along with the noises coming from the rest of the building. Everything disappears but Memphis.

"I'm sorry I wasn't here with you last night. And sorry I didn't reply to your text." I wrap my arms around her and pull her against me, feeling her heart beat against my chest.

"It's okay. I understand. You did what you needed to do. I was fine. Safe." She's trembling, and I rub my hands up and down her back until she looks up at me. "Are you sure you know what you're doing with the police? With Cole?"

I brush a lock of her wig away from her face. "I want to see you. The real you. No more hiding, Memphis. Everyone in this building can know exactly who you are, and not a goddamned thing is going to happen. I won't let anything bad happen to you. I swear it on my life."

"Only if you promise me that you know what you're doing and we're going to ride off into the sunset, holding hands, after this is all over. Swear it to me, Cannon. I didn't find you and fall in love with you just to lose you now. I won't. I refuse to let that happen. I don't care if I have to follow every step you take until this is over. Do you understand me?"

Her eyes turn glassy, and her voice is rough with unshed tears.

"Don't cry, baby. We didn't go through all this to only come this far. You and me have a hell of a lot of memories to make, and we're going to fucking make them." A single tear escapes and I catch it on my thumb. "No tears. You don't need them. Got it?"

She nods and I lower my mouth to catch her lips, diving inside with my tongue, desperate to be closer to her. Memphis's hands come up, and within a few seconds, the wig falls away. She pulls back.

"One second. Let me ditch the contacts. You're right. I'm done hiding. I want to be with you as *me*. Only me."

"Good."

She disappears into the small bathroom and returns with those aqua-blue eyes shining.

"I love you, Cannon, and I swear to God, if something

happens to you, you'd better haunt me for the rest of my life until I can join you on the other side. Don't promise me heaven, then put me through hell. I want a lifetime with you."

"You'll get it. I'll make it happen." As soon as I make the vow, I know there's nothing I won't do to keep it.

CHAPTER
THIRTY-SIX

Our lips collide again. While Cannon is tasting me, skimming down my jaw and sending chill bumps rising, his hands are busy stripping me out of my blouse and bra.

I make quick work of the buttons of Cannon's shirt and pants, until we both stumble toward the bedroom and land on the full-size bed.

"I need you, baby. Right now."

His guttural tone makes me even more desperate for him.

"Let me—" I cut off my words and my lips take a path down his chest as my palms sweep over him. Despite the promises he made me, I have to memorize every bit of his body. Every line of taut muscle and every inch of skin. I'm burning the image into my brain because this isn't just sex.

This is *love*.

I've never felt as beautiful as I do right this moment, with his hands cupping my curves and worshipping me.

When I finally reach his hard cock, I wrap both hands around it and suck the head into my mouth. His groan is the best sound I've ever heard. When the salty flavor of his precum hits my tongue, I revel in it. I take him deep, laving every inch of him, not caring that tears spill from my eyes when he hits the back of my throat.

I want him to remember this for the rest of our very, very long lives together. Maybe it's the primitive part of my brain, but I want him to know exactly what's at stake, and cement every single reason he has to be careful and stay safe.

There's literally nothing I wouldn't do in this moment to ensure this isn't the last time we're together.

Suddenly, Cannon pulls out of my mouth and rolls us both over so he's on top. "I'm not coming in your mouth. I'm coming deep in that sweet, tight pussy that belongs to *me.*"

His possessive words wrap around me, and I've never wanted to belong to someone more.

No, not *wanted* to belong. I *do* belong to him.

And when he pushes my thighs apart and fits his cock against my entrance, I stare up into his hazel eyes and tell him the truth.

"I didn't know it was possible to love someone this much."

"Me either, baby. Not until I met you."

With that, he sinks inside me, stretching me wide, and I arch my back to take him deeper. I want everything he has. Everything he is.

Cannon grips my upper arms and lifts them above my head, threading our fingers together as he pounds into me. Thrust after thrust, he hits my G-spot, and the orgasm builds inside me until I'm teetering on the edge.

"I'm going to come. I can't—"

"Wait. Wait for me. Together. We go together."

He releases one hand and uses his to lift my ass higher, and he powers inside. His thumb finds my clit and with one touch, I'm lost.

"Now," he says.

The orgasm tears through me as Cannon roars my name.

"*Memphis.*"

CHAPTER
THIRTY-SEVEN

I could stay like this forever, still inside Memphis, my head resting near enough to hear her every heartbeat.

But I know I have to get up, and I've never resented a responsibility more. Then I remind myself that once this is all over, everyone I love will be safe. That alone gives me the energy to rise from the bed.

Memphis lifts her head to look at me. "Is it time?"

"Yeah, baby. It's time. Hold on, though. I'll bring you a towel."

I clean myself off in the bathroom and bring her a washcloth dampened with warm water so she can clean up.

While she's taking care of herself, I head out into the small living room to retrieve our clothes. I've got them in my hands when I see an open book with a picture of Giancarlo Rossetti taped to a page. It's on the chair in the corner, resting on top of the laptop that must have come from Dom's office.

"What the hell is this?" I ask the empty room, picking up what I now realize is a leather journal.

The bed creaks, and Memphis pokes her head out into the living room. "What?"

She comes toward me to take the clothes I hold out to her, and I flash the cover at her.

"Well . . . when I started asking questions about the feud, Benny gave it to me. He said all the names were changed, and from what I've read so far, it's like a mob history lesson and then an insider's account of the feud between the Cassos and the Rossettis."

"Benny fucking wrote this? Jesus Christ. Dom would kill him if he knew." *If he weren't already dying,* I add silently.

I drop the journal onto the chair and pull on my pants, but I freeze with my fingers on the button of my slacks when the book flops open to a black-and-white photo of a woman.

And not just any woman.

My heartbeat kicks up and blood roars in my ears as I stare down at Memphis. I jerk my head up to her face.

"What's wrong?" she asks, stilling with both arms shoved through the sleeves of her shirt.

I look down at the picture and back at her. "Why the fuck is there a picture of you in this book?"

"What are you talking about?" Memphis yanks the shirt over her head and closes the gap between us to stare down at the open journal. She stumbles back a step, knocking her shoulder into mine.

I reach out to steady her as I read the caption beneath it.

Selena Mazzini, before she was found murdered in the Mazzini home.

"Why . . . why does that look like me?" Memphis whips her head sideways to stare at me, and all the color is gone from her face. She looks like she's seen a ghost. "Who . . . who is that?"

My teeth grit together, and I reach down to pick up the book.

Selena Mazzini's body was found by her husband, Sonny Mazzini, on the evening of August 12th . . .

I look back at Memphis. "Benny's got a lot of fucking explaining to do."

CHAPTER THIRTY-EIGHT

MEMPHIS

The photo is of a woman who looks like me, but now that I stare at it closer, I see the differences. My eyes are a little bigger and her nose is a bit wider.

But still. It's my face.

I follow Cannon through the brownstone as he yells for Benny. Everyone sticks their heads out of their rooms, and he demands to know who saw the old man last. Tempo directs us to the library, and we find Benny reading in front of the empty fireplace.

As soon as we cross the threshold, Benny looks up from the book on his lap. "You hollering for me?"

"What the fuck do you know that you're not telling us?" Cannon demands, holding out the journal and the picture of Selena Mazzini.

Benny glances at the picture and then at me—sans wig and contacts—and there's not a single shred of surprise on his face. None.

"I told your woman I'd only seen eyes like hers once before."

"On a dead woman named Regina," I add and then jerk my chin toward Cannon. "Is that her real name? Regina Rossetti?"

Benny reaches up and scratches the rough whiskers forming a layer of scruff on his unshaven face. "Yeah. And I'm pretty fucking sure you're the missing Rossetti daughter that Giancarlo and GTR could never find."

My mouth drops open and a coating of ice forms over every inch of my skin.

"No. No. That's not possible. My name is Memphis Lockwood. My father was Leander Lockwood, the reporter and news anchor. I'm not a Rossetti."

"You sure about that, kid? Because Alessandra Rossetti disappeared the night her mother was murdered, and then when Gianni, her daddy, went after Dom for killing his wife, he never said what happened to the little girl. Her uncle and cousins never could find her."

Cannon's grip on my hip tightens, like he's trying to brace me for what's to come, but I'm sure I already know. Still, I ask the question anyway.

"What happened to Gianni Rossetti when he went after Dom for killing his wife?" I swallow the saliva pooling in my mouth, and my entire body shakes as I wait for an answer.

It doesn't come from Benny, though.

From beside me, Cannon says, "Dom killed him. He didn't want to, but Gianni wouldn't listen to reason. He didn't believe that Dom hadn't killed Regina."

"Oh my God." The food I ate earlier rises up with bile from my stomach, and I shake even harder.

Cannon must realize my knees are going to give way, and he maneuvers me into the chair opposite Benny's. "Sit. Jesus Christ, you're fucking white. Benny, get her some whiskey."

"I'll get us all some fucking whiskey," he says.

I hear the chair squeak as he rises, but I don't look his way because Cannon is kneeling in front of me.

"We don't know anything yet. It's just a fucking story right now, Memphis," he says.

But I know differently. I know it in my bones. I know that I'm that missing girl.

"My father would never tell me about my biological mother. Why wouldn't he tell me about her if there wasn't some horrible secret to hide? Like . . . he wasn't really my father, was he?"

Cannon grips my hand, squeezing it so tightly that it hurts, but I welcome the pain. It grounds me. Keeps me from losing my goddamned mind as it feels like it's splintering apart.

"Who the hell am I?"

My lungs heave as he wraps my hand around a glass of whiskey and helps me lift it to my lips. The burn of the alcohol slides down my throat, and I latch onto it as another lifeline.

Everything I thought I knew about who I was . . . is a lie.

Cannon turns his head, and I zero in on the sharp lines of his jaw while he speaks to Benny.

"You fucking suspected, didn't you? And you didn't say

a goddamned thing. Why?" His voice rises with his frustration.

"What the fuck was I supposed to say? She has the same color eyes as Regina and the same lines of her face. I know because I fucking loved Regina when we were young, but her family wanted ties to the Rossettis so she married Gianni. I didn't know your girl was wearing a wig too."

"Then why the fuck would you give her this fucking manuscript? You wanted her to see the picture! You wanted this to happen!"

"So what if I did!" Benny erupts, his face turning red. "If you loved someone and lost them before you could ever have them, you'd want to know what the fuck happened to the last piece of her on this fucking planet. Don't judge me, kid. You haven't lived my fucking life!"

Benny doubles over, a harsh coughing fit racking his body until I fear the old man is going to expire right in front of us, after making this confession in the library.

"Cannon. Cannon." I reach out and grab his hand. "Stop. Please. Don't yell at him."

Cannon tugs his hand from mine and guides Benny to the chair where he was sitting.

"It's okay, Ben. You're okay." He snags a handkerchief from the older man's pocket, and Benny snatches it from him. "Do you want us to call 911? We can get you help."

The coughing slows down as Cannon fishes his phone from his pocket and Benny waves an arm.

"No. No hospital. I'm not spending my last days hooked up to machines while they try to make me comfortable, because there's not shit they can do for me."

"God, Benny. I'm so fucking sorry." Cannon drops his phone on the table between us and kneels in front of Benny. One of his hands rests on Benny's knee and the other one grips mine. "What the fuck do we do now?"

The question may not be directed at anyone in particular, but I answer it anyway.

"We have to find out the truth. I need to know who the hell I am, because if I know my father . . . I mean—" I break off because it hurts my heart not to refer to Leander Lockwood as my dad. He was everything a girl could possibly ask for in a father.

"He was still your dad, baby. No matter what," Cannon says, like he can read my mind, or maybe it's just the sound of the tears in my voice that I'm barely holding back.

And then it hits me.

"What if my dad had that file on Dom because he knew Dom killed my real father and was trying to figure out who killed my mother, because he wanted justice for *her?*"

Cannon and Benny both look at me, and Cannon curses under his breath.

"Fuck. You could be right."

I let the thought marinate in my brain for a few seconds, and pieces lock into place. "He had to have been. It's the only thing that makes sense. And when I found the file, I jumped to conclusions and assumed that he was killed for investigating the Casso family, but I couldn't figure out *why* he was investigating them."

"Wait. Leander Lockwood. The reporter who killed himself in his Upper East Side apartment for no apparent reason?" Benny says, his voice still rough from the coughing fit.

I spear Benny with my gaze. "Yes, but he didn't kill himself. I know he didn't."

"Then who did it?"

Cannon rises to his feet. "We're going to find that out too." He reaches for his phone, but it vibrates before he can lay his fingers on it. His face pales when he reads the message on the screen. "*Fuck.*"

"What?" Benny and I ask in unison.

Cannon meets my gaze like he's afraid of how I'm going to react to what he has to say.

"The Rossettis have your mom. They want to make a trade—for me—in two hours."

CHAPTER THIRTY-NINE

The revelations of the last thirty minutes tilted the axis of my world. No, not tilted. Rearranged it into something I no longer recognize.

I'm pacing as I attempt to collect the smithereens of my world.

Who am I? I can't even devote the time I need to answer the question because we have to triage, and the fact that I could be someone who I've never heard of isn't the most important thing we have to deal with right now.

The only mother I've ever known is in the hands of the Rossettis—the people who have worn the label of "evil villains" in my head up until this point. But now . . . now I'm supposed to believe that there's a chance they could be my family?

The walls of the library and the empty fire grate seem to close in on me until I have to sit. I plop into a chair, and Cannon drops to a crouch beside me.

"Baby, it's going to be okay. We're going to get her back. Just breathe."

I nod, focusing on my clenched fists in my lap. One by one, I force myself to relax my fingers until they're outstretched.

"I'm okay. I'm okay." I repeat the words, as if hoping the more times I say them, the more likely they are to be true. If . . . if I were really Alessandra Rossetti, which I'm *definitely not*, what would that mean?

Visions flash before my eyes of a dark-haired man lifting me into the air, and my flouncy pink princess dress rises and falls with each toss. A woman's voice yells at him from the house to be careful—in *Italian*. But I know what she's saying.

Is it a memory? The picture is so vivid, straight down to the white ruffled socks and the shiny black patent-leather shoes on my feet.

It can't be real. It's not real. I would *know* if Leander Lockwood weren't my father. *Wouldn't I?* But he never told me about my biological mother. Ever.

Why wouldn't he tell me if there was nothing to hide?

I flay myself with questions. Like, *why didn't I push him for more answers? I'm an investigative journalist, for God's sake. That's what I do.* But I already know the answer to that because it's not the first time I've asked myself.

Leander Lockwood was an incredible man, and when he asked something of me, I complied without question. That was the kind of loyalty, confidence, and *love* he inspired in me, the most curious child to ever be born.

But was I born to him?

I had to have been. Maybe he had an affair? Knowing my stepmother for what she is, I wouldn't have blamed him. Although, to hear her tell the story, the tension in their marriage didn't begin until I arrived. *Arrived*, not *was born.*

I always assumed I was a child born to a woman who wasn't his wife and that's why my stepmother treated me the way she did. But I got so much love from my father, it didn't bother me. I was Daddy's girl, and that's the way I liked it. Was I looking for his approval and affection so much that I was willing to overlook all the details of my birth that didn't add up?

Yes. Absolutely yes. And I can't imagine any person on the planet who wouldn't have done the same. My father was *that* kind of man. Magnetic and kind and generous and all things good. Why else would the American people have loved him for so long while he brought them hard story after hard story, but did it with compassion and fairness?

My instinct is to feel stupid and small for not digging, but when I remember my father, it all fades away. There's nothing I wouldn't have done for him. Nothing I wouldn't have refrained from doing.

But he's gone, and I must believe that in this situation, with Cynthia at risk, he would want me to get her back safely. Even though they were divorced, he cared for her and her well-being.

I lift my chin and meet Cannon's gaze. Throughout my pinball machine of a thought process, he's stayed crouched in front of me, waiting for me to digest the information.

"Are you sure you're okay? Because I'd understand if you're not." The way he says it tells me he thinks I am Alessandra Rossetti.

I stare into those hazel eyes that I've fallen in love with over and over, and there's no judgment. No hate. No disgust.

That's the moment I know that he's just as incredible a man as my father. He doesn't see me any differently, regardless of the name and family history I may share with his enemies.

"If I were Alessandra Rossetti . . . which I'm not," I make sure to add so everyone knows where I stand. "Who would the current Rossettis be to me?"

"Giancarlo is your uncle, and GTR is your cousin," Benny says.

I blink a few times as I process the information. "There's no way I'm related to them. There just isn't. I can't be. It's not possible."

Cannon takes my hand between his. "Someone might say the same thing when they find out that Dominic Casso is his father. We don't get to choose our family, baby. No matter how much we might wish we could."

"But they're monsters," I say, my voice breaking when I think of the lives they took and the injuries they caused on the sidewalk with their bullets and the blood they spilled.

"We all are, kid. Some of us just hide it better than others," Benny says.

I cut my gaze to his. "I'm not a monster. I don't care who I am or whose blood runs in my veins, I'm *not like them* or you, if that's what you are."

Benny's face softens, but that doesn't make his next statement any easier to swallow. "If you'd been raised a mob princess, like your daddy had planned, who knows what you might have been capable of. Then again, you could've turned out like Eden. Sweet as pie. We'll never know."

My shoulders tug back until I'm sitting straight up. "My father was Leander Lockwood, and he raised me to be smart, kind, curious, and compassionate." My tone is sharp enough to wound, and Cannon squeezes tighter.

"No one can take that away from you. You're right, it doesn't matter whose blood runs in your veins, you are Leander Lockwood's daughter because he was your father. He didn't have to give you his DNA to make that true. He gave you everything else that made you who you are."

I jerk forward and throw my arms around Cannon's shoulders, tears spilling down my cheeks. "I really want that to be true. I can't take that away from him. *I can't.*"

"You won't. I promise. No matter what happens, I love *you.* I don't care if you're Drew, Memphis, or Alessandra. I don't care which wigs and contacts you wear or how much makeup. I love *you.*"

I pull back and blink while Cannon reaches up to swipe the tears from my cheeks with his thumbs.

"I love you too. But still, I don't like not knowing who I am. I need to know for sure, even if I don't want it to be true."

"Then we'll find out," Cannon says.

"How?"

"I don't think the Rossettis are going to volunteer a DNA sample, but I'm pretty damn sure we can take one after they're dead." The gruesome suggestion comes from Benny.

"We're not killing them, Ben. We'll take them out the smart way, and they'll spend the rest of their lives rotting in federal prison."

The old man hacks and coughs again. "How the hell do you propose we make that happen?"

"I have a plan." Cannon rises and holds out a hand to me.

I stand, staying close to him once I'm on my feet, as if I'm using him as an anchor. Which I am, because nothing else in this room or city makes sense except for what I feel for him.

"We trade me for Cynthia," Cannon says, "just like they demanded."

At that moment, I'm glad I'm holding on tight to him, because the suggestion would have otherwise taken me to my knees.

"No! Not a chance in hell!" My protest fills the room as Benny shakes his head.

"No. I agree with the girl. We have to find another way. They'll kill you."

"And you don't think they'll kill her?"

As soon as Cannon says it, bleak despair fills my chest. *I can't let Cynthia die. No matter what, I'll always love her in my own way. I can't sacrifice her to keep Cannon. But I can't lose him either.*

It's an impossible situation. An impossible choice. The clock is ticking, and I have no idea how the hell we're going to get out of this mess.

I won't lose Cannon. I can't let anything happen to Cynthia.

So, what the hell do we do?

A man fills the doorway and steps inside the room. Cavanaugh Westman, Hollywood's hottest action star. Now that I'm looking, I see the stamp of the Casso family resemblance on his features.

He takes in all of us, giving me a double-take due to my lack of Drew Carson wig and contacts, I'm sure, before meeting Cannon's gaze.

"Fill me in. I might have been out of the game for a while, but whatever the hell is going on, I can help."

CHAPTER
FORTY

Beside me, Memphis clutches my hand, and I can only imagine the battle raging within her. Just like it's raging in me.

The only choice we can make is clear.

I won't let a woman die to save my own ass—especially someone who isn't and has never been involved in the game. She may be a piece of work and a terrible mother, but she's not to blame when it comes to this. I'm not that kind of man, and I never will be.

The Rossettis will kill her . . . of that I have no doubt. They had no problem timing their drive-by to hit the whole family standing on the sidewalk, instead of waiting until it was just the men. They won't hesitate to put a bullet between Cynthia Lockwood's eyes to prove a point.

As for me? They'll kill me too. After they torture me. Or try to, at least.

An outsider might think it's strange that they didn't ask to trade for Dom, but it doesn't to me. He's in the hospital, recovering from a heart attack, which the

Rossettis would already know through their network of informants. There's a reason I left his security with him 24/7. Because I don't trust the Rossettis won't try to off him in his bed.

Dom is an injured animal to them. Not a risk. Enzo's also laid up, which means the most potent threat to their organization is *me*.

I see their logic, even though I think it's flawed. I'm not going to be a gangster, despite what Dom expects of me if I were to take over the family. I'm a businessman, and a hell of a good one. I could easily revamp the family businesses and create more profit from legal activities than Dom does from illegal ones. He's just never given me the opportunity to prove it. And if I turn myself over to the Rossettis, I may never get a chance.

No. I'm not dying today. I'm not going to be another casualty of this bitter feud, which now is finally making sense.

I know Dom killed Gianni Rossetti because Rossetti came to him and accused him of torturing and murdering his wife and tried to kill him for it, even though he'd entered the meeting under the premise of coming in peace. Dom shot Rossetti in self-defense because the man was out of his mind with grief, something that Dom's security should have picked up on before letting the man in the room. Gianni Rossetti had to have already packed off Memphis to Lockwood at that point, because that's the only way he would have taken the risk and truly have nothing to lose. To Dom, I have to imagine it felt a whole lot more like Rossetti committing suicide by rival rather than a murder.

I wasn't there—hell, I was just a kid—but the story spread far and wide, making it clear that the Rossettis and the Cassos couldn't stand one another. And that existed as truth until recently when we started trying to make inroads for peace for the betterment of both families' businesses.

Until GTR Rossetti fucked it all up.

Now we're back to being mortal enemies, and I have to figure out how to survive this day. Because I'm not leaving Memphis. Not when she needs me more than ever, especially because I know that she's Alessandra. You can't look at that picture of Regina Rossetti and not see the resemblance that could only mean Memphis is her daughter.

I don't need a DNA test to believe it. My gut has already spoken.

While my brain is rolling through all of this, I tell Cav what we know. He didn't start working for Dom until I was already gone on my mission to become Creighton's best friend in school. We may not have known each other in this capacity, but Cav did his time working for our father, just like I did. We all put in our time for Dom. And that's about to come to an end.

I hadn't decided to take over the family until this moment, but it's the only choice I can make. I'm done with the bloodbaths and killing.

It ends today.

"What about me?" Memphis says as Cav and Benny discuss options, and I listen.

My passiveness evaporates as soon as her question hangs between us. "What do you mean, what about you?"

"What if you tell them who you think I might be and trade me for Cynthia? It might work. You can't say it wouldn't."

Even as the words leave her mouth, I can see the fear in her gorgeous eyes. She may have war-time experience and been embedded with the troops to bring hard-hitting truths to the masses, but this is different, and she knows it.

"Fuck no. That's not happening. No fucking way are you going anywhere near them. They will never know who you are." My tone is final.

"Actually, that ain't a bad idea," Benny says, and I've never felt the urge to punch him in the face like I do right now.

"No. Fucking. Way." I glare at him, telling him to *shut the fuck up* with my expression.

"That's what your old man would do," he adds.

"I don't give a fuck. I'm not Dom, and I never will be."

"That's the damn truth."

The gravelly voice comes from behind me, and I'm not even sure why I'm surprised that Dom is here. Of course he is.

I pivot and face my father, who, despite having the same voice, looks as though he's aged a few years since I last saw him at the hospital. His ability to show up when I least want him to hasn't changed at all, though.

"You checked out of the hospital against medical advice?"

He nods, his eyes narrowed. "They gave me that whole spiel while I was walking out the door. Like I need a doctor to tell me when I'm ready to go. They don't know jack shit, and I don't take orders from anyone." He scans the room, his gaze landing on Memphis. "I knew you'd look better as a brunette."

Memphis seems to be holding her breath, and I put an arm around her. I honestly don't know how much Dom knows or overheard, but I'm not telling him shit about the fact that Memphis is likely Alessandra Rossetti. It doesn't matter to me, and therefore it doesn't affect him. I also don't give a shit that he'd say the opposite, given the opportunity.

"How she looks as a brunette isn't any of your damn business, and it sure as fuck doesn't impact the situation we have at hand. The Rossettis have her mother, and they want to trade her for me."

Dom's expression doesn't change, and it reminds me of all those times in my childhood when I thought he was a Spartan. So fucking stoic, even when all you wanted to see was a tiny bit of humanity. Since then, I've seen it on his face, like when he sees his granddaughter and he suddenly morphs into a human who lives and breathes and can be hurt.

But not right now.

Right now, he's rock solid.

Dom pins me with a look that would incinerate a lesser man. "The only way they're getting you is over my dead body."

To say that his harsh words surprise me would be a vast understatement. I've never mattered much to my father, and I don't know why he would start caring now. It would take more than a brush with death to change him, because he's had plenty of those over the years.

"Good, because that's what I said," Memphis says, and Dom's gaze dips to her face.

"You have a better idea, girl?" he asks.

"Not yet, but I'm sure we can come up with one. Why does anyone have to be traded? Why can't the cops take them out and rescue her?"

Dom's attention moves to me. "You got a cop who'll get involved?"

His question shocks me, because as far as I've always known, Dom has avoided cops like the plague. He only kept a few on his payroll as a dire necessity.

"I might."

"They got anyone undercover? Inside the Rossettis?"

His question is eerie, and I remember the meeting I had in the club in my office. *Dom has it bugged, and he wants to see if I'll lie to him.* I don't know it for certain, but there's a damn good possibility that he had Primo check the tapes.

"Yes. They've got a man inside."

Dom replies with a sharp nod. "Good, then we let them do the dirty work. I'm not losing you now that Enzo's dead. You're my heir, Cannon. You aren't dying today."

The matter-of-fact reporting of Enzo's death hits us all hard.

"What the hell happened?" I ask as Memphis stiffens beside me.

"Tore some shit open when he tried to leave. Dumbass didn't know how to listen to his body. They got him back on the table, but he didn't make it out of surgery. Why the hell do you think I didn't want to be in the hospital any longer? I wasn't going to give them another chance to try to cut me open."

"What about Creighton?" Cav asks.

"He's being sprung as we speak. He and Holly aren't part of this."

"Good. They don't need to be."

Dom glances at Cav. "You and your woman need to go to Creighton's penthouse. Take Eden and Bishop. I don't want you in the line of fire if shit goes sideways." He looks to me. "Your woman comes with us."

"No. Fuck no." I bite out the reply.

Dom smiles, but it's predatory. "Don't think I don't know everything that happens in this building. I know exactly who she is. Suspected for a while."

His gaze shifts to her. "You can cover your face with makeup and change your eyes and wear wigs, but bones don't lie. You're still the image of your mother, God rest her soul. And I owe you an apology for what happened with your father. Gianni was a good man, a man who was betrayed by his own brother. It's time to take out that piece of shit Giancarlo and his son GTR, because I'm done with this feud. I'm gonna watch my grandkids grow up, and the Rossettis ain't taking that shit from me. I don't care if they're carted off in body bags today or locked up to rot in prison. The bad blood ends now."

From beside me, Memphis trembles as she stares at Dom. "Did you kill my father?"

Dom narrows his gaze. "I just told you I did, girl."

"No, not Gianni Rossetti. Leander Lockwood. The news anchor."

Finally, there's a look of shock emblazoned on Dom's

face, but still, I step in front of Memphis. My instinct is to protect her at all costs. I felt it that day at the construction site, and I feel it now a thousand times more acutely.

But instead of replying with a gun in her face like I expect, Dom laughs. "Fuck no. Not a chance. He was investigating me, though. He tried to be careful, but he wasn't careful enough. A week before he died, he was watching me through the window of Andre's, so I had my guys invite him inside."

CHAPTER FORTY-ONE

"What?" I whisper the question as my entire body freezes.

"Yeah, I met the man," Dom says. "He was all right. We talked for a while, and I told him what happened with Gianni. Told him the truth about what I've pieced together over the last twenty-some years—that Giancarlo had to have killed Regina so that Gianni would come after me, thinking I offed his wife. It was a hell of a plan to take control of the family, and Giancarlo pulled it off. I also told Lockwood I didn't know what the hell happened to that little girl Gianni hid before coming to me, but I wondered if he did."

Shock keeps me standing upright, even though my knees are weak once more. "What did he say?"

"He said I didn't need to worry about that little girl, because she turned out just fine. Better than fine. She was a hell of a woman, and her father would be proud as hell, just like he was."

Tears spill down my cheeks as I blink over and over,

staring at the face of a man who saw my father before he died. Saw him and spoke to him like an equal. A man who definitely didn't kill him, given the respect in Dom's tone and expression.

My voice trembles, and a sob beats my words out. "You liked him?"

"I did. And when I found out he killed himself, I wondered what the fuck happened, because he didn't strike me as suicidal."

I shake my head, a new wave of tears breaking free. "He wasn't. He wouldn't."

Dom nods. "I agree with you. Just like I knew that his daughter, the reporter Memphis Lockwood, who I looked up after the meeting, would come looking to find out what happened to him. I knew who you were the moment I saw you on that sidewalk. You're a chameleon, but you can't hide the bones your mother gave you, Alessandra."

Alessandra. Hearing that name on his lips knocks the wind out of me, because I can't argue the fact anymore.

"I knew too. The moment I saw her. Almost took my breath away," Benny says, turning to Dom. "Today, we end this. That bastard killed Regina. You wouldn't let me touch him for all those years, and I'm done waiting. His death belongs to me."

CHAPTER
FORTY-TWO

CANNON

Memphis, who I still can't think of as Alessandra yet, sits beside me in the back of the Escalade in her Drew Carson wig and contacts. She's here against my wishes. I wanted her at Creighton's, safe and sound, but she refused to let us handle this without her.

"I'll just follow you anyway, so don't try to shut me out."

Knowing how damn stubborn she is, I believed every word she said. But still, I didn't let her come along without rules.

She does what I say, when I say it, and without question. And if anything happens to her, she vowed to come back and haunt me for the rest of my life.

The swap is set to take place in twenty-five minutes, and it'll take us fifteen to get there with traffic.

Cole is on board, along with the team of Feds who have been watching the Rossettis and waiting for the perfect opportunity to take them out. With an active kidnapping of the former wife of a high-profile news anchor, the perfect opportunity is *now*.

Every single person in the car is wearing body armor under his or her clothes. We all agreed that we have a hell of a lot to live for.

Benny's ready. His old gun, the one he used for countless hits but left with Dom when he retired, is loaded and at his side. He made the case for being the one to pull the trigger, because he'll be dead before they could put him on trial for murder. Also, given his condition, there's no way in hell they'll lock him up.

Cole asked for my promise that we weren't coming in armed, and I laughed at him.

"Who the fuck do you think we are?" is the question I asked.

He finally gave up and said that we weren't allowed to shoot anyone who wasn't a Rossetti—in the unfortunate event that things go south—because if we accidentally kill his undercover officer, we'll all be going to prison.

We agreed to the stipulation because we've got fucking better things to do.

When we reach the old warehouse, one that's under construction to become trendy lofts but currently has plastic for windows, I scan for any sign of the cops or Feds. Even though they think they're tricky, they generally suck at staying out of sight. Today, however, I'm surprised to find no signs of them.

Which means they might not be here.

Cole had one more round of approvals he had to get before he could commit his team to the plan, and there's a damned good chance he didn't get the go-ahead. The department has never played well with Dom, and I didn't expect them to this time.

Either way, this ends today. We don't need the cops or the Feds to do what we came here to do.

We circle the warehouse. After cutting through the construction gate, we drive into the wide opening that will eventually be garage parking for residents' use only at exorbitant rates. But right now, only two black SUVs are inside the warehouse's basement, facing the entrance, their high beams lighting the darkness.

Memphis stiffens beside me, and I reach down to squeeze her hand. "Stay right here and don't move. Got it?"

I reiterate the point I made earlier, because the front seats of every one of Dom's vehicles have been retro-fitted to include armor sufficient to stop even a fifty-caliber bullet. The doors are all armored, and the windows are bullet resistant. Basically, Memphis is sitting in a tank that nothing short of a bomb blast could take out.

Right now, Dom rides behind Primo, I'm in the middle, and Benny's up front ahead of Memphis.

As soon as we come to a stop, the doors of the other SUVs open. Giancarlo Rossetti and two of his goons—one of whom must be the undercover—step out of the back doors of one. Out of the other SUV come GTR, Cynthia, a junior Rossetti cousin, and someone who makes Memphis suck in a harsh breath.

"What the hell is Randi doing here?"

I follow her pointing finger to the black-and-silver-haired woman standing behind GTR.

"I have no fucking idea, but that doesn't make any sense," I reply, but Dom doesn't have any such confusion.

"She must be expendable, and they're using us to take her out because they're done with her. They think they're smart, but they're fucking stupid. Come on, it's time to do this."

Our doors open and the four of us climb out, but not before I crush my lips against Memphis's.

"I love you. No matter what happens next, I will love you forever."

"Danger, don't you dare fucking get shot. Promise me."

I can't give her that promise, so I kiss her again and follow my father.

My palms itch for the two pistols tucked into the compression shirt covering my body armor, and I wonder if I've been lying to myself about this all along. Maybe I am a gangster and I didn't know it.

Then again, the only person I want to take out is Giancarlo, for killing Memphis's biological mother. And if my suspicions are right . . . in a roundabout way, he might have killed both of her fathers too.

It's the only explanation that makes sense about what happened to Leander Lockwood.

Dom told him what he suspected about Giancarlo killing Regina, and if Leander was anything like his daughter, he would have shifted his focus to the Rossettis. Which means there's a hell of a good chance that it got him killed. It wouldn't be the first time the Rossettis have staged a murder as a suicide, and for that, I want vengeance.

They've taken too much from the woman I love, and it

ends today, in this warehouse basement with water dripping from the pipes and the scent of destruction in the air.

"Surprised to see you still standing, Dom. You really are Teflon, even when it comes to bullets." Giancarlo taunts Dom for what is certainly going to be the last time.

Beside me, Benny stands casually, but only a fool would dismiss the old man as not being lethal. I have no idea how many people he has killed, and I don't want to. Suffice it to say he's paying his penance because he doesn't have long on this earth.

"Give us the woman. We're not here to fuck around," Dom orders.

Giancarlo laughs. "Didn't think you'd be so quick to turn over your kid in exchange for this annoying bitch, but I guess I shouldn't be surprised. It ain't like you don't have more of your bastards hanging around to fill his shoes once he's dead."

It might upset others to hear someone speak of their death so casually, but Giancarlo's attempt to rile me doesn't work. I learned my ice-cold expression from the best—Dom and Creighton.

"You should've picked better. This one's always been disposable." Dom jerks his head at me.

I don't even feel the slash of his words, because I know what he says isn't true.

Giancarlo's laugh shifts in my direction. "How could you be loyal to this prick, kid? And trade yourself for this cunt? I wouldn't. Guess you really don't have balls, Cannon. Come over here so we can show you how we handle someone who doesn't have any balls."

In the past, I would have cared what they said. But

now I know it doesn't have a damn thing to do with me, and everything to do with Giancarlo. He's been trying for the last twenty-five years to prove he deserved the position he stole, and yet he still feels like a fraud. No wonder his son turned out to be such an asshole too.

"I don't fucking trust you any further than I could throw your fat ass, Rossetti," I holler at him. "So send her over, and when she crosses the middle, I'll come to you."

Giancarlo shoves Cynthia forward. As the woman stumbles toward us, gaining speed with each step, Randi's hand appears with a flash of metal. Thoughts fly through my brain with rapid-fire speed.

Fuck. She's got a gun.

Maybe we misjudged her, and she's the one who's going to snipe Cynthia before she can get to safety.

We didn't plan for that, and I don't think anyone else sees her piece.

Shit.

I charge forward, catching everyone off guard, and even though I can't see them, I know every hand is reaching for a gun. I plow into Cynthia and tackle her, and we go down as bullets start flying. One grazes my ear as I drag her with me, heading for refuge behind a concrete pillar. But before I get there, something burns across my arm.

"Police! Everyone lower your weapons," a voice calls over a bullhorn as cruisers with flashing lights roar into the garage.

"You motherfucking, double-crossing—" Giancarlo levels the barrel of his gun on Dom's chest, but not before Benny's aim finds its mark and the man's head explodes.

As GTR lifts his weapon to fire on the cops, Randi presses the muzzle of her gun to his temple.

"Not so fast, you fucking asshole. You're under arrest for murder, along with being a giant fucking piece of shit masquerading as human, and for having a tiny dick and not knowing how to use it. You have the right to remain silent . . ."

As Randi begins her colorful recitation of GTR's Miranda rights, Cole rushes forward, and cops and Feds swarm both the Rossetti party and the Cassos. Benny is handcuffed, and Dom is too.

Memphis jumps out of the SUV and rushes toward me and Cynthia. "Oh my God, you got hit! We need an ambulance! Someone get an ambulance!"

"It's just a scratch, baby."

"Don't tell me it's just a scratch!" Memphis wraps both arms around me and holds on tight.

Cynthia stares at us in shock. "I want to go home. I'm never coming to New York again."

"I'm glad you're okay, Mom."

Cynthia bursts into tears, and Memphis tries to calm her while Cole walks over to me.

"That's not exactly how this was supposed to go."

"One dead and one wounded. I think it went just fine."

He glances from me to Dom, who stares at Giancarlo's body and his brains splattered on the concrete.

"I'm done with this life." My father grunts, tugging at his handcuffs. "It's time to fucking retire."

"You can retire in prison, Dom," Cole tells him.

My old man laughs. "Haven't you heard? I'm Teflon. Nothing sticks to me."

EPILOGUE

CANNON

Six months later

Benny passed peacefully in his sleep four months after the shootout with the Rossettis, and we gave him a wake that would have made him happy as hell. The entire family toasted his life and his death at Andre's, all wearing Hawaiian shirts in his honor.

Before he died, Benny and Memphis turned his journal of a manuscript into a book, and with Dom's blessing, he published it. Benny told us to make sure we added *author* to his epitaph. Every single person who came to the wake received a copy, and given how things are going with the book's sales, there's a damn good chance we'll be adding *bestselling author* to his epitaph instead.

Even though Cole got his arrest with Dom, he didn't get his conviction. Once again, Dom walked free. Cole was pissed for a second, but it didn't last long since he got his big promotion with GTR's conviction. The entire

Rossetti organization fell apart, and its pieces were gobbled up by the other crime families.

Randi got a promotion too, and she's now a bona fide detective. She even assisted in reversing the official report on Leander Lockwood's death. Now the world knows the truth about Memphis's father, and justice has been served. After the insurance policy paid out, Memphis donated it to start a scholarship to journalism school in her father's name.

Dom, true to his word, officially retired shortly after he was released from police custody. He handed me the reins and told me to do whatever I thought was right. Then he seduced the nurse, Judith Maria Hansen, bought a place in Boca, and convinced her to run away with him.

Cynthia went to rehab, terrified that the Rossettis were able to so easily grab her because she was hammered at the bar of the Plaza. She and Memphis are taking it slow with their new relationship. Even though they don't share blood, they share a bond that they're carefully rebuilding.

Teal graduated from rehab as well, and she and Grice are now in a happy, committed relationship. Tanya has never been happier either, since she has taken over a large portion of my management role at the club like she was meant for it.

I stand in the brownstone in Hell's Kitchen, consulting with a design team as we create a brand-new vision for the building Dom gifted me—affordable housing for single mothers, complete with a day-care facility that's included in the cost of rent. *I owe it to you, but also to your mother. Do something with it that she'd like.* We're still working out the details, but Creighton is consulting on the project with me. As a matter of fact—

I glance down to check my watch. We're going to be late for dinner with him and Holly if we don't get moving soon.

I thank the team and go find Memphis in the library, the one room that won't be altered because she made the request. She got her DNA test, and she is indeed Alessandra Rossetti, but she's decided she won't ever use the name. Memphis was given to her by Leander, in honor of his hometown, and for that reason, she'll use it forever. With one change, though—she's not going to be a Lockwood much longer. Soon, she'll be Memphis Freeman, my wife.

I stand in the doorway, watching her work, hunched over a laptop at a wide wooden table she's turned into her desk. She's so engrossed in what she's doing that I don't want to break her concentration, so I take a step back. A creaking floorboard gives me away, though, and her head pops up. When she sees me, she slaps a hand over her chest like I almost gave her a heart attack.

"Holy hell, Danger. Sometimes I forget how quietly you can move."

"Lifetime of practice," I tell her with a laugh. "I was going to let you keep working, but . . ."

She checks the clock on her computer and shoots up from her seat. "Oh shit. It's time to go, isn't it? And you were going to let me keep working and make us both late?"

"When you're in the zone, I'm not going to be the man to pull you out."

A flash of sadness flits across her face before she says, "I just got through a tough part, so I'm ready."

Memphis writes true crime now, having given up being an on-air reporter for good, but her investigative spirit is still fully engaged. Her first book untangles the story behind the murder of Regina Rossetti. It's been hard on Memphis, but she's determined to get the truth out there for everyone to know, because her mother deserves the honor.

I hold out my hand. "Then let's go."

***

"Have you set a wedding date yet?" Holly asks Memphis, checking out her ring once more.

I proposed three weeks ago, over Italian food and wine. Well, not actually *over*. I snagged an extra-small pizza box from Geno, filled it with notes with just a few dozen of the reasons I'm madly in love with her, and settled the ring on them. When Memphis opened it, her aqua eyes shimmered with tears. Then I read her every single note before finally popping the official question. Thankfully for me, she said yes instantly.

Memphis glances at me. "Not yet. We're still talking about what we want to do."

"Knowing Cannon, he'll try to talk you into running away and doing the deed somewhere in secret," Creighton says, like he lives in my damn head. The man still knows me better than anyone.

Memphis tries to hide her smile because she and I have been debating whether we want to do it up traditionally, or if we want to keep it small and intimate. As in just the two of us on a remote beach somewhere.

"But if they do that, we won't be able to be there," Holly says, her mouth forming a small moue.

I shoot her a look. "I didn't get to come to your wedding."

As Creighton's laugh booms in the restaurant, Holly narrows her eyes. "Different situation, Cannon, and you know it."

"If you're looking for somewhere exotic," Creighton says, "we've got friends in Ibiza. The Forges own an island."

"Or you could do it in New Orleans!" Holly's face brightens with a look of pure glee. "Eden has a whole crew of friends, and it would be awesome! You could do the parade through the French Quarter and everything."

Through it all, Memphis is quiet, a small smile on her face as she toys with the ring that's been newly added to the fourth finger of her left hand. When I suggested catching a flight next week to the South Pacific and getting married, just the two of us, her eyes lit up with excitement. I know what my girl wants. Even if it's not traditional, it's perfect for us.

Memphis's gaze lifts to mine, and I see that same anticipation on her face now as she speaks. "We'll let you both know when we decide. Promise."

After dinner is finished, and the women have hugged and said their good-byes and we've helped them into my Bentley and Creighton's new Rolls Royce Cullinan, my brother and I stand on the sidewalk facing each other.

"You're not getting married in Ibiza or New Orleans, are you?" Creighton asks me.

"Not if you let me borrow one of your jets next week."

Creighton shakes his head at me. "You would fucking do that."

I shrug, but a smile tugs at one corner of my mouth. "I'm doing whatever the fuck she wants for a wedding. Dom's in Florida. You and Holly are heading back to Tennessee. Cav and Greer are in LA. Eden's in New Orleans—"

"And you don't want to wait to make Memphis yours," Creighton says with a crooked grin of his own. "I get it. I really fucking do. If that's what you want, I'll make sure there's a long-haul jet fueled up and waiting on the tarmac at Teterboro when you need it."

"I appreciate that, brother. Because I'm not waiting any longer. I'm ready. She's the one. No need to wait and plan all the stuff. I just want to go do it and make her mine."

"Then that's what you'll do. I'm fucking happy for you, Cannon. Really damn happy. You deserve it. But you better believe that we're throwing you a hell of a reception when we can get the whole family together after you get back. It's happening."

"Fair enough."

He holds out his hand and I take it, leaning in to give him a back-slapping hug. Having Creighton back in my life means the world to me. It's like regaining a missing limb.

As we separate, I notice a man walking up the sidewalk toward us in jeans, a dark hoodie pulled up over his head and obscuring his face. I reach for the piece tucked into my waistband, but he hits the pool of light cast by the streetlight just behind my Bentley and lifts his head, revealing a familiar face.

"I ain't gonna jump you. Not when I've been hoping like hell I'd run into you both. And now here you both are, like fate put me in your way," Gabriel Legend says, pushing back his hood.

Creighton puts himself between Legend and the Cullinan—just like me, always moving to protect his woman first.

"What the hell do you want, Legend?" I ask the man as he shoves one hand in his pocket. The other looks like the knuckles are busted, and he flexes it as if he just walked away from a fight.

His shakes his wild mane of hair free from where it's caught in his hood and lifts his chin. "Got a business proposition for you. Opening a new club."

Like the underground club he owns where Teal got in trouble, I'll bet.

"Casso family is clean. We're not interested," I tell him.

Creighton stays silent, as if answering is beneath him because it's ridiculous to expect he'd give money to the street fighter turned illegal club owner.

"No. Not a dirty club," Legend says, shaking his head. "A high-class one that'll attract every celebrity in town, especially the ones who can't get into your damn cigar bar."

"You're going legit? I don't buy it," Creighton says, his tone rife with skepticism.

Legend lifts his chin at me. "Cassos did it. Shouldn't be so hard to believe."

"Sounds like a bad investment to me," my brother says, pushing back at Legend.

"What if I'm willing to pay you back at double the market rate?"

I gotta give the guy credit. He's asking the right people. If he could get our money behind his club, he'd have no problem attracting more investors.

"You that sure it'll succeed?" I ask him.

"Yeah. Fuck yeah, I am. I'm doing this, with or without investors. I got a plan, and it's not gonna fail."

Knowing what I do about clubs in this city, I should disagree with him. But he already runs what I understand is one of the most profitable underground enterprises in the city. Although going legit is a different proposition altogether, some part of me is still intrigued.

"Ask me again after I get back from my wedding in a few weeks," I tell him, stepping toward the back door of the Bentley.

"Might not need your money by then. You don't want to miss out on Urban Legend."

"Apropos. I just hope you don't end up as one," Creighton says and then nods at me. "I'll talk to you later, brother. Congratulations."

Legend lifts his chin at both of us before tugging his hood back over his wild hair. "You'll see. Both of you. Just wait."

He continues down the sidewalk, his stride long and rangy, and his posture forbidding enough that no one would dare try to jump him. I don't know his story, but I have a feeling it's a dark and gritty one.

Pushing any more thoughts of Gabriel Legend out of my mind, I slide into the back of the Bentley and wrap my arm around Memphis.

She curls into my side. "Who was that?"

"No one important. The real question is . . . how long do you think it'll take you to find a dress?" I press a kiss to the crown of her head.

She turns her face to look up at me. "Are we really doing this? Like, soon?"

"As soon as you're ready, baby. Just say the word."

A grin spreads over her face. "This is New York. I can be packed and ready to go in forty-eight hours."

I cup her cheek with my hand. "Perfect. Then let's go make you Mrs. Freeman."

Memphis

Two days later, we climb out of the SUV next to the jet on the tarmac, and nerves flutter in my stomach like butter-flies. *We're eloping. We're really, really doing it.*

But that's not why I'm nervous.

Warren opens the door and I climb out, waiting for Cannon. He takes my hand and threads our fingers together.

"You ready for this, baby?"

I simply nod because I'm afraid if I speak, my voice will crack and he'll know something's up.

Warren unloads our luggage, and the crew meets him on the black-and-white Karas International rug that leads us up to the stairs. By the time our luggage is swiftly stowed and my feet touch the KI logo, I'm about to burst with the secret I've been keeping.

Please, please be happy I did this.

Cannon gestures for me to go ahead of him up the stairs, and I give the flight attendant a quick smile. Her grin is *huge.*

I slip by her into the cabin . . . and spin around so I can see Cannon's face when he realizes what I've done.

His expression is *everything* when he sees the jet packed with his family—Dom and his new lady love, Creighton and Holly, Cav and Greer, and Eden and Bishop.

Complete shock.

Absolute awe.

Overwhelming happiness.

He drops his gaze to me. "How? Who?"

"Creighton and I did it," I say as tears fill my eyes. "I hope you—"

Before I can finish, Cannon sweeps me up into his arms and crushes his mouth to mine. Everyone erupts with cheers and claps and laughter.

When he finally sets me down, his hazel eyes glisten. "I love you so fucking much, baby. *Thank you.* Now this is perfect." He scans over my shoulder once more, taking in all the people who love him, before squeezing me tighter against his side.

"I hope you're all ready for some fun and sun, because we're going to get married!"

THE END

Curious about some of the other characters who appeared in the Dirty Mafia Duet? You can find Creighton and Holly in the Dirty Billionaire Trilogy, Cav and Greer in the Dirty Girl Duet, Logan and Banner in the Real Good Duet, and Bishop and Eden in *Beneath These Shadows*. You don't want to miss out on their stories!

Defiant Queen

Sinful Empire

SAVAGE TRILOGY:

Savage Prince

Iron Princess

Rogue Royalty

BENEATH SERIES:

Beneath This Mask

Beneath This Ink

Beneath These Chains

Beneath These Scars

Beneath These Lies

Beneath These Shadows

Beneath The Truth

DIRTY BILLIONAIRE TRILOGY:

Dirty Billionaire

Dirty Pleasures

Dirty Together

DIRTY GIRL DUET:

Dirty Girl

Dirty Love

REAL GOOD DUET:

Real Good Man

Real Good Love

REAL DIRTY DUET:

Real Dirty

Real Sexy

FLASH BANG SERIES:

Flash Bang

Hard Charger

STANDALONES:

Take Me Back

Bad Judgment

ABOUT THE AUTHOR

Making the jump from corporate lawyer to romance author was a leap of faith that *New York Times*, #1 *Wall Street Journal*, and *USA Today* bestselling author Meghan March will never regret. With over thirty titles published, she has sold millions of books in nearly a dozen languages to fellow romance-lovers around the world. A nomad at heart, she can currently be found in the woods of the Pacific Northwest, living her happily ever after with her real-life alpha hero.

She would love to hear from you.
Connect with her at:
www.meghanmarch.com

9 781943 796335